Whose Hand?

Whose Hand?

A Skeeter Hughes Mystery

Judith Yates Borger

Nodin Press

Acknowledgments: This book would not have been completed without help from my friends, who offered encouragement, criticism, background information and copyediting. Just a few to whom I owe gratitude are Vicki Olson, Claudia Kittock, Margaret Francis, Kristin Bolden, Sujata Massey, Gary Bush, Stan Trollip, Maureen Fisher, Susan Hilt, Betty Lasorella, Ellen Hart, Lisa Bullard, Elissa Mautner Nolting, Tony Palumbo, Richard Stelzer, Andi Larsen, John Toren, and Lisa Friedland.

Of course, my husband, John, and adult children Jenni, Chris and Nick never cease to feed my soul. None of my family, however, is represented in any way in my mysteries.

I'd love to hear from you. Please email me at Judy@JudithYates-Borger.com or visit my website http://www.JudithYatesBorger.com for more information.

Photos and book design: John Toren

Library of Congress Cataloging-in-Publication Data
Borger, Judith Yates
Whose hand? : a Skeeter Hughes mystery / by Judith Yates Borger.
p. cm.
ISBN 978-1-935666-05-9
1. Women journalists--Fiction. 2. Murder--Investigation--Fiction. 3. Minnesota--Fiction. I. Title.
PS3625.A82W56 2011
813'.6--dc22

2011003806

Nodin Press, LLC
530 N. Third Street,
Suite 120
Minneapolis, MN
55401

for Jenni

I studied the crags in the old man's wind-burned face. His gold and silver hair was pulled into a ponytail at the nape of his neck, leaving his bald head open to the elements. The ragged collar of a black T-shirt peeked through the v-neck of a dirty blue-green sweater with a run in the left sleeve. Nicotine had stained the dirty fingernails on the left thumb and forefinger he used to grip his ceramic coffee mug.

Leaning a little forward in his chair, he looked me straight in the eye, the stench of his breath hot in my face. He rubbed his left hand on the thigh of his faded camouflage pants—the green kind from a jungle war, not the sand-colored ones from a desert war. He told me he was fishing in Lake Harriet on one of those warm, sunny days last October.

"My butt was getting numb," he said, "but I cast off one more time, and sat a bit longer. Then I felt a little tug—like maybe I'd caught milfoil. There was weight but no wiggle, ya know what I mean?"

"Yeah, I do." I'd fished some with my daughters.

"But that was no fish that broke the surface of the water." His crow's feet grew deeper as he broke into a smile, then pushed the coffee cup aside with the back of his hand, as though he didn't want it to come between us.

"It was someone's hand," he said.

Chapter 1

Minneapolis, Minnesota
February 12

He said it loudly, with a combination of shock and mirth. So loudly, in fact, that the guy sitting at the next table looked up from his computer. Then the old man leaned back in his chair, which gave him a better perch to watch my reaction.

"A hand?" I asked. "Are you sure it was a hand?"

"Yes, ma'am."

This was one rough guy, I thought. Should I believe him? I wasn't sure, but it couldn't hurt to listen. I reached in my purse, pulled out a pen and my long skinny notebook with the spiral at the top, and flipped it open to the first page. "Start at the very beginning."

He'd fished Lake Harriet several times a week for years, he said, and had even caught muskie late in the fall. This time he'd been lowering his line all day long with no luck, until the big catch.

"I tried to reel the thing in. A big ol' airplane was coming in low over the lake just then, making such a racket I couldn't think straight. I leaned over a little too far, I guess. I was holding the pole with one hand and reaching with the other and the blessed thing slipped through my fingers."

"Meaning the hand, or the pole, slipped through your fingers?"

"Both. I lost my new Shimano Baitrunner reel my boys gave me for my birthday."

"What did it look like?"

"The reel? It was a beauty."

"No. I mean the hand."

"Oh, it looked like a human hand, but it had been in the water a long time, I figure. All bloated and kind of mushy looking."

"What did you do?"

"I shouted a word I wouldn't repeat in front of a pretty lady like you. A sight like that can really jack up a guy's ticker, if you know what I mean."

"I can imagine. Then what? How long did it take you to reel the hand in?"

"Quite a while. Must've come from deep water. The lake can get eighty or ninety feet deep, ya know."

"Was there a ring? Tattoo? Anything?"

"All I saw was some of that milfoil hanging on it."

We were meeting in Linden Hills, a neighborhood on the west shore of Lake Harriet. The coffee shop, in what had been a neighborhood drug store, was adjacent to a women's boutique in what had once been a used bookstore. A couple of women chatted quietly on a black leather couch. It was the kind of place where a good conversation was better than a month of therapy, and a lot cheaper, too.

"Is this your usual place?" I asked, unable to imagine him as a regular here.

"Hell, no," he said. "But I've lived in Linden Hills my whole life."

"How's that?"

"I grew up just a couple of blocks from here. Long before it became so dee-zire-able. Couldn't afford to buy a house here now. But I like coffee and I figured a high-falutin' newspaper reporter like you would like a place like this."

The cappuccino maker hissed along with the soft jazz playing in the background. I was trying to formulate the next question, but I kept wondering why the owner of the adjacent dress shop wasn't worried about coffee spilling on her merchandise when an open sliding door invited customers to float back and forth between the two establishments. Maybe I was subconsciously avoiding the gruesome image.

"Was it a right hand or a left hand?" I finally asked.

"Ma'am, I was so shook up I didn't take the time to figure that out."

"All five fingers?" I asked, trying to suppress a grimace.

"Looked to me like all the parts were there."

"Know anybody who fell in the lake recently?" I asked.

"Nope."

"Heard any stories about anybody losing a hand?"

"Nope."

"Got any idea whose hand it might have been?"

"Beats me."

I glanced over to the next table and noticed a teen apparently doing homework online. I live near the coffee shop and recognized her. She was the daughter of a friend of mine. She wore white earphones and seemed to be bouncing to a beat. I wondered what class she was taking, and whether my girls would be doing the same soon.

"Did you drop a buoy marker?"

"No," he said, shaking his head.

"Did you try to get a visual marker, like line up where you were with a house along the shore?"

"I was pretty shook up, so I just rowed back into shore. On my way I passed a guy who was taking his sailboat out of the water for the season. They have to have all the buoys empty by the end of October. Anyways, I told the guy what I saw and all he said was, 'Is that so, Pop?' Imagine. He called me 'Pop.' Like I'm too old to be believed."

"Did you call the cops?"

"Yeah. But I think they don't believe me. Even my boys think I'm crazy, but I swear on my beloved wife's grave, that's what happened."

I wasn't surprised he had trouble getting people to believe him. Sometimes it's hard to separate the story from the rheumy eyes and tremulous hands of the teller. Urban myths about sunken treasure and six-foot-long fish have been floating around Lake Harriet for decades. I wondered if this was just another one. What's more, he claimed this happened last October. We were meeting in February. Was this a fish tale that had grown over five months?

"I hope you won't take any offense at this next question, but I can't help but notice you seem to have a cataract in your right eye. Are you sure you saw a hand, and not something else you mistook for a hand?"

"My right eye may be a bit cloudy, but my left eye is twenty/twenty," he said.

"I know there have been times when fishermen have sat in their boats all day long just drinking beer. Are you sure you didn't see a fish that looked like a hand?"

He pulled back from the table, his face awash in disappointment. Then he looked me dead in the eye and with great earnestness said, "I pulled a hand out of Lake Harriet."

I gave him my card and suggested that he call me if he thought of anything else. He promised me he would and rose from the table, absentmindedly pulling at the crotch of his pants before reaching for his hat and scarf. We shook hands and he gave me a sly wink before ambling out the coffeehouse door.

People like to tell me stories. Sometimes on the phone. Sometimes in coffee shops. Sometimes in their homes. I always listen, but skeptically. Each time, I try to figure out if the storyteller is just another nut looking to get his name in the newspaper, or the real deal. I listen because that's my job. I'm a reporter for the Minneapolis *Citizen* and my beat is missing persons.

As I watched BJ trudge down the sidewalk, his heavy rubber boots leaving big prints in the newly fallen snow, I decided I believed his story. Don't ask me why. Maybe it was intuition. Maybe it was my reporter's DNA. Something told me the story was more than some old codger's fish tale. Turns out, I was right.

Chapter 2

"Hey, Hughes. What ya got for me today?"

That's Thom Savage, my team leader. He would tell you he's the reason I have this job, and I guess he would be at least partially right.

A generation ago, Thom would have been called an editor. That was before the newspaper industry fell ill. Today most adults who grew up on *Sesame Street* and *MTV* are not picking up newspapers for sports, entertainment, education, public awareness or anything else. Meanwhile, the few news junkies there are don't need to wait for their favorite newspaper to land on their doorstep to find out what's going on. One click on the Internet to any of a zillion news sites can tell them more than they want to know about any news event—no charge. Sometimes it's true, sometimes it isn't, but not enough people seem to care about the difference. It's no wonder that fewer and fewer people look at newsprint—or the advertisements that pay for it.

The folks at the top of the journalism food chain have been going through all kinds of contortions trying to stave off obsolescence. One idea was to change the titles of everyone except reporters. Hence, Thom became a team leader instead of an editor, even though the bulk of his time is spent editing.

The rest of the time he's under tremendous pressure from managers above him and reporters below. Those on top want him to fill the paper every single day with interesting, informative—and true—stories that people will want to read. The people below him want to write those stories, but they usually want the time to do them well, or at least adequately. That costs money the newspaper's shareholders don't have. To stanch the red ink, many papers have fired staff—a lot of staff—which means there are fewer reporters to fill the newspaper's pages with scintillating stories. Some, like our paper, have filed for bankruptcy. It's a pressure that can harden a lump of coal into a diamond, or crush a human spirit into dust. I sometimes wonder what it will do to Thom.

I had been in the newsroom all of twenty minutes after meeting with the old man. So far, I had nothing for Thom, story-wise.

"I just talked to a guy who said he fished a hand out of Lake Harriet," I said.

Normal people might have found that shocking, but not Thom. He just thought the story sounded, well, fishy.

"It's February," Thom replied. "The lake is one giant block of ice. Did he catch this while ice fishing?"

"It happened last October, before the lake froze."

"What's that got to do with a story? Your job is missing persons, not missing hands."

This particular beat, one of a slew that management started in the last few weeks, was Thom's idea. He argued that assigning a reporter to chase missing persons would be a public service, especially if the newspaper managed to find someone the cops could not. And besides, people love to read and wonder about lost folks, particularly kids. The brass bought the idea.

"This beat was a tough sell," Thom reminded me yet again. "If we don't produce enough 'missing' copy you may end up back in the suburbs, covering the next Taco Bell opening. There probably isn't another newspaper in the country that has a reporter assigned full-time to missing persons. Remember that, Hughes."

Hughes. That's me. My name is Skeeter Hughes. Until last month, I covered Land o' Lakes, a wealthy suburb just west of the Twin Cities. In my last assignment I found a missing eighteen-year-old girl. Although it was the week from hell, my work did catch the eye of the top bosses and gave Thom the idea for this beat. The combination was my ticket out of Land o' Lakes.

Always impeccably dressed, Thom's white shirts and navy slacks are crisply pressed and he has a tie assigned to each day of the week. I've long suspected that his partner, Bob, with whom he lives in a 1960s suburban rambler with their two kids, does his ironing for him.

My new beat is a risky move for Thom, career-wise. He's very bright, aggressive and articulate, and chooses his battles wisely. He's a master at managing those above him on the food chain. Better, in fact, than managing those below him. Even though he still struts around the newsroom like a man in control, I've noticed an increase in the twitch in his left eye.

"So…do you think you'll have the story for me today? The budget is looking a bit light for tomorrow."

The budget is a list of stories scheduled to appear in the paper sometime in the next few days, weeks or even months. Each story has a name called a slug, and three or four sentences describing what the reporter expects to deliver. Editors—or team leaders—with light budgets get testy.

"I doubt I'll be able to come up with a missing person from the lake in time to make tomorrow's newspaper," I replied. "But I figure if he caught a hand, minus its body, there might be a missing body minus its hand to go with it."

"Tell me what you've got so far," he said, the eye-twitch taking an extra leap.

I filled him in on my meeting with the old man.

"How did you find him?"

I love it when an editor asks me that question with a note of incredulity in his voice. Makes me feel like I'm some kind of a hot-shot reporter. The truth is, however, that I met him because one of his sons, on whom I'd had a crush in the seventh grade, had called me. But I wasn't going to tell Thom that.

"I have my sources," I replied.

"Do you believe him?"

"It's a pretty fantastic tale, and he could just be loony tunes, but, yeah, I believe him."

"I don't know, Hughes. Remember the story about the sophomore at the University of Wisconsin who said she was abducted?

Everybody was hot for that story until it turned out to be a fake. Even CNN looked bad for chasing it. All it's going to take to kill this missing person's beat is a big story about a person who isn't really missing."

"C'mon, Thom," I replied. "I'm not going to get the Lindbergh kidnapping every time. But people actually go missing. That's what made this beat so attractive. There's plenty to work with."

Before I landed this job I used to look at posters stapled to street posts by people looking for their loved ones. I sensed there was a story behind every disappearance. A basket of riches, at least from a reporter's point of view.

He had no reply, just walked away, shaking his head and muttering something about a press conference the governor had scheduled. He was almost to the next reporter seated down the line when he stopped, turned around.

"Hughes. I need a story I can put in the paper, soon."

I nodded acknowledgement as I wondered how I could most efficiently get him the story he needed. If the Goddess of Good Stories was with me, I could make a couple quick phone calls, figure out who might be officially missing—and missing a hand—and have a story for him by, say, tomorrow. Boy, was I wrong. The Goddess was apparently embedded in Afghanistan and not checking her messages.

Chapter 3

I slipped on my phone headset and called Sergeant Victoria Olson, a police officer with whom I had worked from time to time in Land o' Lakes. She'd taken a job with the Minneapolis Police Department just days before I began the missing persons beat. I hoped she'd be able to connect me to a body to go with the Lake Harriet hand.

"Sergeant Victoria Olson," she answered with her usual gravelly, no-foolin' around voice.

In my mind's eye I saw her standing at five-feet, eleven and a half inches, feet spread shoulder width apart like the roots of an oak tree.

"Skeeter, here. Nice to have you working in Minneapolis. I was wondering if you had any reports of people who had been missing since sometime last fall."

"This is the hello I get?" she replied with a deep chuckle. "No 'how are you?' Reporters sure do get to the point. Why are you looking for a missing person in Minneapolis? I thought you were the queen of Land o' Lakes."

"You gotta keep up with the times, Victoria. That's old news. I'm now mistress of the missing. Glamour girl in search of the gone. Desperate for the disappeared."

"Yeah, well, I'm still Sergeant Olson," she replied. "And you're still a reporter looking for news. Now as far as missing people, you happen to be in luck, because that's a small part of my new job, and I was just getting acquainted with the files this morning."

She said police were actively looking for three people who had gone missing in the fall. A black female, age eighteen, reported by her grandmother last August. A white female, age thirty-six, also last seen in August. A white male, age seventy-five, last seen sometime late summer.

"We're not sure how long he's been gone. His wife reported him missing in November, but they're apparently estranged because she said she last saw him sometime in late September."

"Gee, Sergeant, that's not very many for a state of five million people," I replied.

While we talked I fingered the leaves on the poinsettia plant on my desk. Someone had sent it to the newsroom over the Christmas holiday and I adopted it. I read somewhere about a woman who threw the dregs from her coffee cup in an office plant at the end of every day to save herself a trip to office kitchen sink. Much to her surprise it flourished. I'd been trying the same and this one was doing amazingly well for February.

"This isn't for the whole state. It's just Minneapolis," she replied. "And as you know, lots of people go astray without getting reported missing. What's your interest?"

I debated whether to tell her the hand-in-the-lake story. Sergeant Olson and I have had a tenuous relationship. When she wants the public's help in finding a killer, for example, she's as pleasant as can be. And when I need to tell the public about crime nearby, I'm very agreeable to her. But when she doesn't want people to know something, and I do, or I fear she may interfere in something I'm working on, we're not so friendly. In this case, I needed to run the hand story by her, to test whether my buddy BJ was telling me the best of all fish stories. Her reaction to the tale surprised me.

"I heard one of the other officers talking about that old guy's story." The timbre of her voice was as low as a man's. "Even if it's true, what are we supposed to do about it? He's got no hand for us to investigate."

Unfortunately, I was in the same spot, but I was still trying to find its owner.

She went on to say that while the missing persons reports were part of her job, they were a low priority. I asked her if I could look at the reports.

"They're public record. Look all you want," she said.

The *Citizen*'s newsroom makes its home in the old Grain Exchange building, connected by tunnel to police headquarters, which takes up half of Minneapolis City Hall. The easy access to both, no matter the weather, or, say, a nuclear blast, is a definite plus. I grabbed my notebook, took the elevator down to the basement and trotted past the huge gray sandstone blocks that line the musty passageway under Fourth Street.

Up half a dozen well-worn marble stairs is the 1902 Father of Waters Statue, carved from Carrera marble from the same Italian quarry used by Michelangelo. I took a quick right, then went into the police department records room on the left.

"Hi, Skeeter," Elissa Mautner, my favorite records clerk, said. "What hot news are you looking for today?"

"Victoria Olson said there were three 'missings' reports. I'd like to take a look."

"That would be Sergeant Victoria Olson," she replied. "Our newest officer?"

"The very one. What do you think of her?"

"Of course, it would be impolitic of me to say anything less than glowing about her," Nancy replied with a wink. "But I will say there was some speculation about her before she arrived."

Nancy leaned through the wooden half door that separated the records department from the hallway and lowered her voice. "The word is she was fired from Land o' Lakes."

"Why?"

"For harboring a girl she was supposed to be looking for."

I had asked her the question not to learn the answer—which I already knew—but to test the quality of Nancy's gossip. As usual, it was dead on. "Can I see the incident reports for the three missing people?"

She disappeared back into the catacombs of files and returned moments later with three sheets of paper, containing only the sketchiest of information. Typical, I thought. Rarely do the cops release the juicy stuff the first time a reporter asks.

"How about the supplemental reports?" I flashed my biggest, sweetest smile.

"Now Skeeter, you know the supplemental reports aren't available until the case is closed," she said.

"You can't blame a girl for trying." I signed the log.

The missing seventy-five-year-old white male was one Yuri Yudeshenka, a furrier originally from the former U.S.S.R. Caucasian, five feet, two inches, 120 pounds. Although his estranged wife listed his business address in the warehouse district of downtown Minneapolis, she said he had moved to Anoka, a town about twenty miles north and west of Minneapolis.

Mostly rural, but increasingly citified, Anoka is a microcosm of the changing America. Rumor has it that the Russian mafia has operated a thriving business in endangered species there for years, because the residents don't believe in sticking their noses into other folks' business. For the same reason, it's a great location for cooking up methamphetamine, which occasionally sends a split-level rambler sky high. I imagined all kinds of gruesome scenarios that would make Yuri a candidate for the missing hand.

Pace Palmer was reported missing by a coworker after she failed to return from a two-week vacation in late September. Palmer oversaw human trials for medical devices produced by a company based in Plymouth, a suburb just west of Minneapolis. Her coworker said Palmer was white, thirty-six years old, five feet, eleven inches, 130 pounds.

The young woman, Amber Thomas, was described by her grandmother as five feet tall, about 100 pounds with a tattoo on her right arm. Although she lived with her grandmother and five siblings, grandma worked nights as a nursing home attendant and Amber was normally gone much of the day. Amber had been missing since August.

As I carefully wrote the pertinent information in my notebook, it occurred to me that these were all light-weight people. Maybe that's hazardous to one's health. All the more reason to skip the diet that was always in my future.

Not a bad catch for an hour's work, I thought. The first week on the missing person's beat and I had three possibilities. Any one of them, or none of them, could be without a hand. I felt a smile grow on my face. This was going to be fun.

Chapter 4

For the more complicated stories, like this one, I often keep a log of calls, noting the phone number, the time and the name of the person I'm hoping to reach. If I make contact on the first try, which seldom happens, I mark the entry with a check. If not, I write LM—for left message. Sometimes my list of calls can run on for pages, but the log can come in handy when I'm on deadline and can't quite remember exactly whom I've called.

I had no idea if, or even whether, any of these leads would pan out so I headed back to the newsroom and placed calls to the three who had reported the missing people. In about five minutes I marked LM next to the entries for Yuri's wife, who was with a customer, Pace's boss, whose voice mail said she'd get back to me "just as soon as possible," and Amber's grandma, who, according to a girl who sounded way too young to be home alone, was grocery shopping.

Ten minutes later my phone rang.

"Skeeter Hughes," I answered with my left hand, while clicking off the competition's website with my right.

"I'm returning your call about Amber," the woman on the line said. "I'm her grandma, Gladys Johnson."

Mrs. Johnson said Amber had last been in her house in early August. It was hard to understand her as she spoke over the racket of a crying baby and a TV game show, but it was something about Amber turning eighteen she didn't have any say over what Amber did.

"I did my best with that girl," she said ruefully. "But I've got the other children to look after too."

"You're obviously a busy woman," I said.

"I am. But I like to look people in the eye when I talk to them. Could you come to my home to ask your questions?"

Most reporting is done over the phone because it's quicker. But she sounded like a nice lady, so I agreed. She gave me her address.

Half an hour later, I pulled to the curb in a tired neighborhood in south Minneapolis, pushed my way through a rusted chain link fence, then climbed the cracked concrete steps to the lower level of a duplex badly in need of painting. Plastic trucks poked through the snow. Two boys and a girl who looked to be pre-school age all answered the doorbell together.

"Hi, I'm Skeeter Hughes. Is Mrs. Johnson here?"

The three looked at me suspiciously for about a minute. "Do you want my sister?" the oldest finally said.

"OK," I said, thinking that maybe an older sibling would lead me to their grandma.

The boy disappeared while the other two kept watch over me. When he came back minutes later he was carrying what appeared to be a month-old baby.

"Here," he said, handing her over to me.

"No, no, no," I said waving my right forefinger. "I'm not here to take your sister. I'm here to talk to Amber's grandmother."

A woman came to the door, and put her hand on the boy's shoulder. "What are you doing, child?"

"Looks like somebody wants to give a baby away," I said with a chuckle, then offered my hand. "I'm Skeeter Hughes."

The police report said Amber's grandma was fifty, but this woman looked at least seventy. And she and the children were all dark-skinned African Americans. Hmmmm. BJ hadn't said anything about the race of the hand he pulled from the lake. I had assumed it was white. I suddenly flashed on an editor who once said, "A reporter should assume nothing, except maybe a two-per-cent mortgage."

"I'm Gladys Johnson," she said, pulling the baby tight in her arms. "She cried all night. I think she kept her older brother awake. Come in."

I stepped into a small living room. The furniture was worn but clean. There were lace curtains on the windows and I smelled a ham in the oven. "Turn off that TV now, Tyesha, while I talk to this reporter," Mrs. Johnson said to a girl in an adjacent room. "Take the baby, please."

Tyesha turned off the TV, threw the remote on the couch a little more forcefully than necessary, then took the infant.

"What can you tell me about Amber?" I asked after we were seated.

"She's always running with her girlfriends. Couch hopping."

I'd never heard of that before. "Cow shopping? What's that?"

"That's what I thought the first time I heard it, too," Mrs. Johnson said. "Couch hoppers sleep where ever they can find an empty couch."

She had reported her granddaughter missing in an effort to get rid of bill collectors who were hounding her. "I pay my own bills. It's not easy but I do it. But I won't be responsible for that girl's bills, especially now that she's eighteen."

"You talking about Pinky, Grandma?" Tyesha shouted from the other room.

"Yes. Now you mind that baby," her grandmother replied gently.

"Pinky?" I asked. "Do you call her Pinky?"

"The kids call her Pinky because she was born without her right baby finger. But to me, she's Amber."

"She seen trouble," she said. "Her daddy came and went and her momma, my daughter, has passed. I told her over and over, 'Amber, wear life like a loose garment, child.' But I don't know if she heard me. She always seems so attached to things, you know? Her clothes, her phone, her friends. But she always got her schoolwork done. Been attending college classes since she was a junior in high school through that program for smart kids. She's supposed to graduate from Minneapolis South High School in June. Got a full scholarship to the University of Minnesota. Says she's going to study architecture."

"A full ride?" I asked. "Good for her."

Mrs. Johnson launched a huge smile, her chest raised in pride. She had good reason. Half the kids who start Minneapolis public high school drop out.

The baby let loose a wail that about shook all the pictures of kids off the walls. "She's hungry again, Grandma," Tyesha called.

Mrs. Johnson excused herself as she went to feed the baby, which left Tyesha with me.

"Sounds like Amber is a smart girl," I said to Tyesha.

"Oh, she smart alright," Tyesha said. "She plenty smart."

"Sounds like there's something more about Amber," I said.

"Amber's always watching. She watched her girlfriends and remembered," Tyesha said.

"Meaning … ?"

"Meaning she saw that the girls who went to school every day, did their homework and played sports seem … happy."

"What did she do with that knowledge?" I asked.

"She played basketball in winter and soccer in spring, summer and fall. And she didn't have babies. "

"You sound like you're proud of her," I said.

The clock on the mantel ticked away half a minute before Tyesha answered.

"We're lucky because we got our Grandma. But she don't know everything about Amber."

"What doesn't she know?"

"Amber wasn't always playing basketball and soccer," Tyesha said.

"Oh… what else was she doing?" I asked.

"You sure ask a lot of questions," Tyesha said. "You a newspaper or TV reporter?"

"Newspaper. What was Amber doing when your grandma thought she was playing sports?"

"You like Lois Lane?" Tyesha made it clear she wasn't going to tell me anything more about Amber.

"Not really," I said. "She's just in movies."

"I'm eleven. I want to be a reporter when I grow up."

Although the print industry is dying fast, there will always be a need for honest, savvy journalists who can analyze information and deliver it through whatever means the future holds. Tyesha was obviously self-possessed, an important trait for a journalist. I invited her to the newsroom for a tour.

"TV reporters are cooler than newspaper reporters. But it would still be cool," she replied. "Yeah, I'll do that."

Mrs. Johnson returned to the room while burping the baby on her shoulder. Tyesha told her I had invited her to the paper.

"Can I go, Grandma?"

"We don't want to take advantage of the lady," Mrs. Johnson said.

"No problem," I said. "How about Friday?"

"That's very kind of you, Miss Hughes. But tell me, why are you asking about my Amber?

I explained about my job, but left out the hand-in-the-lake part. She didn't need to hear that. "What's Amber's dad's name?"

"Davis. Davis Thomas. Amber's father moved to Florida after her mother passed on. Orlando, I think. That was five years ago and we haven't heard from him since.

"Maybe Amber left town?"

"I never heard Amber say anything about going after him, but you never know with kids."

I doubted whether she had a phone number for Davis Thomas, but asked any way.

"If I did, I'd be looking for some support from him for his babies." Right on cue, the baby spit up on Mrs. Johnson's shoulder.

While she wiped up with a clean, cloth diaper, I looked at her quietly and wondered. If her daughter had died, and Davis Thomas had split, to whom did the newborn belong? Not the three kids who answered the door, and I figured Tyesha was too young to be the baby's mom. I did the math in my head. If Mrs. Johnson had a child at fifteen, and her daughter had a child at fifteen, and that child had a baby at fifteen, she could easily be a great grandma.

"Whose baby is that?"

"Amber's younger sister's," she said, adding that the last time she saw Amber was August. They fought because Mrs. Johnson planned to take the baby in. Amber had left angry, shouting that if her sister was old enough to have a baby she was old enough to take care of that baby herself.

"I love that girl like my own daughter." Mrs. Johnson's eyes began to tear up and I found myself trying to keep mine from doing the same.

I understood that visceral pain that haunted Mrs. Johnson at the thought of Amber being in trouble, or worse, dead. If one of my girls was missing, I don't know that I could even function, let alone carry on the everyday tasks of running a household, going to work, taking care of other children.

"She's got a future, you know," Mrs. Johnson said. "I'm so afraid that something terrible has happened to her. "

"I'll let you know if I learn anything about where Amber might be," I said.

"Thank you, dear," she said. "You seem like the kind of person who cares."

I left my card with her, said my goodbyes and drove back to the newsroom, thinking about everything I had learned about Amber Thomas. She was poor, lucky and smart, all accidents of birth. She was poor because her mama passed when she was nine years old, the victim of high blood pressure and diabetes. It didn't help that mama was overweight, overworked and had too many babies. And, it didn't help that daddy didn't help, her grandmother had told me. As Tyesha had said, she was lucky to have a loving grandma, and she was smart because she used the intelligence God gave her.

Amber would be the first in her family to go to a four-year college. If she were still alive, that is.

Chapter 5

Back in the newsroom, I drummed my fingers on my desktop, wondering where to go next. One of the biggest challenges facing newspapers is reaching younger readers. At the same time he proposed my "missing person's" beat, editor Thom suggested the paper assign a reporter to write full-time about issues important to eighteen to thirty year olds. Management bought that idea, too, and gave the job to a 26-year-old guy who had grown up in St. Paul and graduated from the University of Minnesota. If anyone would have an idea on how to track down Amber, he would, I figured.

"Hey, Jay," I said, sidling up to his computer. Jay Novak, wearing jeans, a T-shirt and tennis shoes, looked nineteen. On his tall days he stood all of about five feet, six inches. The rumor in the newsroom was he really wanted to be a sports reporter, but took this job as a way to work on the paper. He was well known to hit the bars with the sports reporters after deadline. He didn't look up.

"Hey, Novak!" I shouted in his ear.

"Yo, Skeeter," he replied, quickly closing the page on his screen. He'd been so involved reading the latest issue of Sports Illustrated online he apparently hadn't heard me until I raised my voice. "What's happening?"

I asked him about how I might try to track down Amber.

"At any given time there are about a hundred couch hoppers in each of the city's high schools," he said. "What's the kid's name, again?"

"Amber. Amber Thomas. A girl. They call her Pinky because she's missing her baby finger."

"Couch hoppers skip town all the time. Your buddy Amber may have bagged a train or a bus and left for good. But I'll keep an eye open."

I mumbled thanks and ambled back to my desk, almost tripping over the duct tape that covered tears in the carpeting every few feet. Was Jay right? Did Amber skip town? I didn't know and wasn't sure how to find out.

Because she was African-American and missing a pinky finger, Amber's hand would be the easiest to identify, I figured. With luck, the hand my new buddy pulled out of the lake would have also been missing a pinky and my work would be done for me. I dug out his number and made a quick call.

"Hi, there, Skeeter. Did you find the body?" I heard the volume drop on a television game show in the background.

"Not yet, but I have a question for you. Could you tell the race of the hand you pulled up?"

"You know, I've been thinking about that," he replied. "I'd really like to help a pretty lady like you. But I just couldn't tell. It was mushy."

"Could you tell if all its fingers were there?"

"When I see it in my nightmares it always has all five fingers," came the reply. "Why do you want to know that?"

I explained about Amber's finger.

"I told you I couldn't tell if it was a right hand or a left hand. So even if it had all five fingers, it could have been the other hand."

"You're right," I replied. "I was hoping for a lucky break. Thanks."

"Call any time," he said. "I like talking to you."

Thom loped over to my desk in the newsroom just as I was unwrapping my Quiznos chicken sandwich. "Whatcha got for me today, Skeeter?"

I took a quick big bite, and because my mouth was full, I had a couple beats before I had to answer. "Still tracking down possibles to go with the hand," I mumbled. "I'm not going to have anything for you today."

To make sure he knew I was actually working, I filled him in on my morning with Amber's grandma. "I'm looking for Amber's father," I said.

I checked Dex Online for a Davis Thomas in Orlando. Nothing turned up, which didn't really surprise me. Next I checked the news morgue for the Orlando Centennial, one of our sister papers. I asked the search engine to go back seven years and pull up all the articles it could on Davis Thomas. Unfortunately, the paper's sports writers apparently couldn't stop writing about a basketball superstar with the same name at Orlando's Oak Ridge High School. There were more than a hundred mentions of his name but I found nothing about the Davis Thomas who was Amber's dad. I checked a dozen more of our sister papers. No luck.

Maybe I was wasting time chasing Amber, I mused. Tyesha had implied Amber had another life her overworked grandma hadn't discovered. Maybe Amber was fed up with being a good girl and just blew town.

Or maybe the hand belonged to Pace Palmer. But the little I knew about her made me think she wasn't the type. I couldn't remember a time when someone involved in the medical device field was personally tied to something so gruesome. Yuri, on the other hand, so to speak, seemed a more likely candidate for foul play than Pace. Still, I was puzzled.

I was beginning to feel that familiar gnaw, the need to produce something, soon. And it was only Monday.

Chapter 6

If I couldn't find Amber, maybe I could find a way to eliminate her from the possibly handless. I wondered if the race of flesh that had spent some time in the bottom of a beautiful lake would be apparent.

I logged onto the search engine at the University of Minnesota, Twin Cities campus. They've got an expert for everything over there and I figured there would be someone who could tell me what a hand without a body might look like.

I scrolled through a list of pathologists until I came across the name Emerson. I recalled recently reading that he was involved in some high-profile case, although I couldn't remember which one. That meant he was accustomed to talking with reporters and likely a good source. I called.

"If you come to campus right now, I can talk with you," he said.

The Minneapolis campus of the University of Minnesota, my alma mater, lies just east of downtown, about a forty-five minute walk from our newsroom. Although it would have been healthier to hoof it—when had I last exercised?—I decided to drive because I still get a thrill driving my sexy little red convertible, even if it wasn't the original one I bought new.

It had taken me weeks of checking online every day to find a 1995 Honda Civic del Sol to replace mine that had been firebombed last month, but I finally found one in Cicero, Illinois. I flew into Midway Airport, met the seller in the parking lot with a check, got the keys and drove it home. It had a bigger engine and

20,000 more miles on it than my old one had, but it was red and in excellent repair. Most important, it felt good, like my car. I turned up the radio and sang all the way back to the Twin Cities.

On a sunny winter day like this one, the two-minute drive across the Mississippi River to the east bank campus is both charming and uplifting. Something about the sparkling of the Mighty Mississip' always touches the Huck Finn in me, making me want to build myself a little raft and head off on a great adventure. Today's adventure was tracking down Dr. Dan Emerson, M.D., Ph.D.

The University of Minnesota is huge. Most students commute. Still, parking on campus is a nightmare. After crossing the river I headed east on Washington Avenue and took a left on Harvard Street, to the parking ramp adjacent to the Radisson Hotel Metrodome, where I snagged the last open spot. Reporters with an expense account can afford to park there. Students can't.

Feeling safe within a phalanx of students, I dashed across Washington Avenue, against the light, and made my way to the Mayo Memorial Building, built in the early 1950s when the University of Minnesota medical school was pioneering heart-related surgeries. When I was in college I didn't really care that the world's first successful open-heart surgery, the first use of a heart pacemaker, the first artificial heart valve all got their start here. It didn't matter to me that by the 1960s the work had spawned several small medical device companies.

In the nineteenth century Minneapolis became a leader in manufacturing prosthetics after a lot of workers lost limbs in the milling and logging industries that grew up around St. Anthony Falls. By the end of the twentieth century, Minnesota in general, and the Twin Cities in particular, was a hotbed for new and improved body parts, an industry that has made many Minnesotans mighty rich. If you were going to lose a hand, this was the city to do it in.

I took the rickety elevator to the basement in the Mayo building and hung a left down a long corridor lined with sea foam green subway tiles. About every fifteen feet a tile had a piece missing at just about the height where many a runaway gurney had gouged the wall. I followed the tiles until I came to an open office door.

Dr. Dan Emerson was sitting on a wooden swivel chair at a scarred wooden desk no doubt original to the building.

"Looks like you found your way okay," he said when I rapped lightly on his door. "Come in, Skeeter. Take a seat in my Shangri-La."

Nothing illuminated by fluorescent lights can ever come close to Shangri-La as far as I'm concerned. The guy's eight-by-eight office was "decorated" with shelves screwed into the walls to hold Mason jars of pickled appendages. I caught myself staring at a long, thin, tangled piece that looked like a foot-long emaciated white worm.

"That's plaque that I teased out of an artery to the heart," he said proudly. "Impressive, huh?"

"Uh, yeah." It was all I could do to muster a reply while trying not to think of the buttery spaghetti noodles I had had for dinner last night. I got right down to business, explaining about the old man and the hand in the lake.

"Is there a way to tell how long it might have been there?" I asked.

"The normal changes of decomposition of a body are delayed in cold, deep water so bodies may be surprisingly well preserved even after a long period of immersion," he said. "These conditions also favor the formation of adipocere, which—"

"Adipocere?"

"Adipocere is the transformation of the fatty layer beneath the skin into a soap-like material. The process requires many weeks or even months."

Is this a great beat or what? I thought as he talked. I never would have learned this if I were a business reporter. "Would a hand that had been under water that long hold any pigment?"

"What do you mean?"

"I mean, would you be able to tell the race of the hand?"

"No," he said. "Pigment or hair on the knuckles, for example, would be the first to go. Plus, it would probably have bugs on it. And in shallow waters turtles love to nibble on things like that."

I suddenly flashed on the pet turtles—Tommy and Tammy—that my girls released into the lake a few summers ago. Had I known that was what the little snappers would be doing I might have talked the girls into keeping them in their bedrooms instead.

"Is there any way to tell why a hand would be found, and not a whole body?"

"Suicides sometimes tie their hands or feet together," he said. "As the body decomposes sometimes an appendage separates at the point where it was tied."

Suicide. I hadn't occurred to me that the hand might be the remains of a suicide. That would mean no story here. The paper only reports suicides when they're very public or someone famous. That would mean that I had spent all this time on a story we wouldn't report. Thom would not be happy.

"How do you tell if someone died from suicide or homicide?"

He leaned back in his chair, heaved a sigh and folded his hands in his lap.

"Homicidal drowning is uncommon, because it requires that the assailant be bigger than the victim, or the victim must be incapacitated by disease, drink or drugs. Guns, poison, or knives are much more reliable means of murder."

"And suicide?"

"An autopsy may show evidence of other suicide methods such as drug overdose or slashing of the wrists," he said.

Unless a body floated to the surface when the ice went out on the lake, there would be no autopsy, I realized. Was there any story here?

"What if someone was killed elsewhere and the body was dumped in the lake, weighted down?"

"It's happened," he said.

"What if the hand of a dead body were tied to some kind of anchor then thrown into the lake? Might the hand dislodge and break away?"

"That's certainly possible. But if the rest of the body were not weighted down it would float to the surface pretty fast. Gases build up in the gut."

"I hadn't thought of that," I replied.

"Didn't you tell me on the phone that your beat was missing persons?" he asked.

"Yes."

"Then I suggest you get to work finding the person missing from the hand."

I gave him my card, thanked him for his help then headed for the parking ramp. Someone had taken something sharp—a key, perhaps?—to carve a big X on the trunk of my little red del Sol.

"Shit!" I shouted to no one in particular as I kicked a rear tire.

Chapter 7

Having hit a dead end looking for Amber, I turned to my call log and started dialing again. Another LM for Margaret Anderson, Pace's boss, and Katya Yudeshenka, who reported Yuri missing. While I waited for them to call me back, I ran name searches through the newspaper's database to see if anything had already been written about the missing three. Neither Amber nor Pace showed up, but a colleague, Nancy Ison, who had since gone on to the Los Angeles Times, had done a profile on Yuri ten years ago. It was a lengthy piece, giving me insight into Yuri that I might not have gotten otherwise. I read it carefully, twice.

Unfortunately, the youngster who would be named Yuri Yudeshenka looked much older than his years when he was a boy. So when the Nazis burst into his quiet home in the darkest of nights in January 1944 they thought he was 14 years old, instead of 10, and hauled him away along with his father and brother to Majdanek concentration camp in the Polish city of Lubin just past the Russian border. The first prisoners of the camp had been political dissidents, but in the spring of 1942 it became a death camp for Jews, Poles, Germans, Russians and a few Americans. They were rounded up and transported like trapped animals whose fate rested in the hands of their captors.

Yuri saw his father, who was elderly, and his sickly brother quickly dispatched to the gas chamber and then the ovens made from the chassis of old trucks and fueled by coke. The ovens were just long enough to hold two men, head to foot. Years later, Yuri prayed that his father and brother had been together at their end.

One bitter cold day Yuri found himself working beside a man of about 30 who was strong, healthy and spoke with an accent Yuri had never heard before. The man was a Russian-born American Jew who had come to the area in search of pelts for his furrier business when he got caught in the Nazis' net. After their eighteen-hour day of labor they shared a wooden bed with two other men. Yuri heard stories about camps where the skin of Jews was used to make lampshades. When Yuri cried at night, the man held him as his father had, stroking his head, trying to soothe away the horror of their lives.

Months later, as they slept in their clothes and wooden shoes so no one would steal them, the man whispered in Yuri's ear, "Don't be afraid. We'll be freed soon."

On July 23, 1944, just seven months after the Nazis kidnapped Yuri, Soviet troops liberated Majdanek. The Russian-American, Saul Yudeshenka, adopted Yuri and with the help of the American Red Cross they sailed for America.

Saul knew other furriers who made good lives for themselves in America. But Yuri had another idea. They went to Minneapolis. The city wasn't as big as New York or Chicago but it was big enough, and colder. The season for wearing furs was much longer.

Saul taught him the furrier trade, and Yuri had a good living, working from the walkout basement of his house on the south end of Lake Harriet. He liked the furs, liked the smell, the feel of the oils on his fingers. He refused to work with the pelts of endangered animals, but had no problem with animals raised for the purpose of making coats, hats, gloves and purses. After all, those animals were farmed, like oats or corn.

Decades later, long into the night, Yuri put out his filter-free Camel cigarettes in the glass ashtray inscribed with furrier supply company Rubenstein/Ziff's logo and thought back on how his fortune had changed from his days in Majdanek.

Leaning down to the drawer in his workbench, he pulled out his bottle of Cognac and poured more in the snifter. He needed a little sustenance to get him through this special order.

As he made a pattern for the mink pieces to be sewn together, he talked about his wife, Katya, a quarter of a century his junior and still a handsome woman. He marveled that she married a small bald man with a thick accent such as himself. She was well suited to handle the retail end of the operation and did a fine job.

Because of the Nazis, Yuri had no trust in banks, he said. "Trust in God and everyone else pays cash," was his motto.

Yes, life was good, he said as he lit another Camel. His only desire was to die a natural death, surrounded by his family.

The piece came with a picture of Yuri at his workbench. I printed it out to pin to the cloth covering of my cubicle, thinking that I needed to come up with photos of Amber and Pace, too. Then I made a second round of calls. Still no Margaret Anderson, but Katya Yudeshenka answered the phone with a gravelly "Furs of Siberia."

"I was looking at a police report of missing persons today and saw that your husband is missing," I said after identifying myself. "Could I talk with you about that?"

She said she was with a customer and would call me back when her assistant returned from lunch if the store wasn't too busy. "I really don't care if the bastard ever comes back," she said, matter-of-factly just before she hung up the phone.

She didn't say she wouldn't talk to me. She just hung up. Maybe it was a lost connection, maybe the building was on fire, or maybe somebody who wanted to spend a million dollars on furs had just walked in, but I wasn't going to be put off that easily. I called back.

"Talk," she said.

"I noticed that your store is in the Warehouse District, just a few blocks away from the newspaper. Can I come over?"

She told me I could stop by but we would have to talk between helping customers. "We have our end-of-season sale going on right now. Maybe you'd like to look at a fur. I have some lovely pieces still available at a very good price."

I had to stifle a smile. If I came home with a fur coat, or even a fur hat, the girls would fall over laughing. My idea of fashion is tacking a daughter-made painted macaroni pin on my chambray shirt. The last time I wore a skirt was my wedding, I think.

Establishing rapport with a source is rule number one in

journalism so I had to make her think I was interested in more than just the sordid details of her husband's disappearance. That would be tough. I'm not one to join up with People for the Ethical Treatment of Animals and throw fake blood on mink-wearing passersby, but I don't like to see animals treated badly, either. Fur coats fall on the abused animals side of the line, in my book.

"I'd love to take a look at what you have, Mrs. Yudeshenka," I replied. Didn't mean I had to buy.

Furs of Siberia was born half a century ago in what's still called the Warehouse District of Minneapolis because, well, the six-square-block area is a warren of warehouses. At the turn of the twentieth century goods brought in by barges and rail on the Mississippi were stored in the warehouses that lined the river. What the area lacked in cleanliness it also lacked in charm. Home to big, dirty hulking buildings, the warehouse area offered a lot of crummy, cheap property with a great view of the mighty river.

By the turn of the twenty-first century when most of the warehouses had gone vacant, the area went through a renaissance. Instead of storage for car parts, farmers' tractors, and sacks and sacks of grain, developers began to turn the space into lofts and condominiums. Overnight denizens went from the homeless to homeowners, with Audis and the occasional Prius, who loved twelve-foot, floor-to-ceiling windows and concrete floors. Best of all, they had views of the river only rats had enjoyed for years. I had to hand it to the Yudeshenka family. When the value of the property sank to its lowest they bought three more warehouses, then watched the value of the properties shoot up faster than a river bluff.

I pulled out of the ramp adjacent to the Grain Exchange and took a quick left on Fifth Street, then headed left again on Washington Avenue until I got to First Street, just past Hennepin Avenue. As luck would have it, there was a space available directly in front of the furrier. I only had two quarters in my purse, enough to buy half an hour. If Mrs. Yudeshenka was especially gabby I'd have to interrupt her and ask for change, then run out to drop more quarters in the meter. Not something I wanted to do. But I didn't want to get a parking ticket either. I've tried to expense them before and the newspaper's cheapskate accounting system always kicked them back. And that was before the budget got so tight.

The wood on the outside of the building was a pocked forest green that probably had stories of its own to tell. I walked through a windowed door to a small vestibule and suddenly faced iron bars with a keyed lock that looked serious. The woman behind the bars waved me in with an expression that said 'don't mind the bars.'

"Mrs. Yudeshenka?" I asked.

Two older men punched hand calculators at desks littered with coffee cups behind a partition just to the left of the door. One chic woman was reading the morning paper. Another, wearing white hair and blue smock, ran a sewing machine as someone spoke in Russian from an area behind them all.

"Yes," said a woman with short spiky pumpkin-colored hair who looked about forty. She was tall and thin with alabaster skin and eyebrows darker than the sable vest she wore. Her lipstick matched her hair. "Can I help you?"

"I'm Skeeter Hughes."

Her smile faded just a bit, but not completely. Maybe she figured there was a chance that she might sell me a coat.

"Yes, let me show you around," she said with a sweep of her hand and a hint of her Russian accent. "Please follow me."

I scooted past a whole zoo of furs, some dyed neon green, others shocking pink. If there was any chance that I would buy anything from this place before, it was dashed when I spied a Barbie doll dressed in a tiny orange fur coat. The price tag was $150. I wondered if that included the Barbie.

"Were you interested in a vest or a coat?" she asked.

"The coats are lovely, but my primary interest is your husband."

"My estranged, soon-to-be ex-husband," she corrected me.

She looked around furtively and glanced over the top of a rack of full-length fur coats, giving me the distinct impression that she didn't want anyone to overhear our conversation. I thought that odd, considering there were no other customers in the store. But then, maybe she didn't want any of the other workers to eavesdrop.

"Why do you care where he is?"

Now that was a curious first question, I thought.

"I write about missing persons. I saw that you reported him missing to the police. I'm following up."

"That's more than the police did," she said sarcastically. "Yes, I reported him missing, but I made the report because the life insurance company told me I had to if I was going to collect anything on the bastard. It's holding up the divorce, but I suppose I can wait if it means I might get something out of the marriage."

Isn't she a charmer, I mused.

"I take it you didn't get along with Mr. Yudeshenka. How long were you married?"

"Fifteen years." They had no children, she said.

"When and where did you see him last?"

"In my lawyer's office at the beginning of the summer."

"You were working out the details of the divorce?"

"I was trying to. He wasn't."

"What was the sticking point on your divorce?" Sometimes I'm amazed at the personal questions reporters ask. If somebody asked me that question, I'd tell her it was none of her business. But apparently Katya didn't feel that way.

"The animals."

"The animals?"

"Yes. The animals. He wouldn't part with them and neither would I."

"What do you mean you 'wouldn't part with them'?"

"I mean the furs are worth a great deal of money." She stroked the sleeve of a full-length sable. "What did you think I meant?"

"I thought you meant you had some emotional bond with them," I replied.

That drew a throaty laugh that ended in a small cough. Definitely a smoker, I thought.

"Yuri is in love with animals. I'm in love with money."

She went on to say she had worked with furs since she was a little girl in Novi-Sibirska in Siberia, where her parents were furriers. She met Yuri on a wholesale shopping trip.

"He said he loved me. I didn't love him, but he was my ticket to America."

"Did he ever spend any time near Lake Harriet?"

"We lived on the lake."

Maybe fifty or sixty homes circle Lake Harriet. By anyone's definition, they're all mansions. Some are four stories high with turrets and multiple balconies. Others are simpler boxy affairs made of brick and stucco. Each is impeccably kept, usually by Hispanic-owned lawn services. They tend to turn over more frequently than houses farther away from the lake. I've always guessed that's because CEOs, whose jobs come and go with the rise and fall of their stock values, tend to live there. It's an upscale, transient neighborhood.

"The police report says Mr. Yudeshenka lived in Anoka."

"That's where he moved after we separated," she said. "I still live on the lake."

She gave me the address, which I copied down. I made plans to check the value on the house and whether the taxes were paid up. As I wrote in my notebook she cocked her head to one side and squinted at me as though appraising a sable.

"Why are you really interested in Yuri?" she said.

Figuring it was time to 'fess up, I answered her with a question. "Have you heard anything about anybody finding anything unusual in the lake?"

"Unusual? Like what?"

"Like something a fisherman might have pulled out."

She noted the lake is pocked with ice houses this time of year, and allowed as how she could not imagine why anyone would want to sit on an upturned bucket all day long holding a fishing line over a hole in the ice. I had to agree with her on that point.

"If people are stupid enough to do that they're welcome to whatever they pull out," she said.

"I'm not talking about ice fishing," I said. "I'm talking about before the lake froze. Sometime last fall."

"Ms. Hughes. I have no idea what you're talking about."

"I'm talking about a fisherman who says he pulled a hand out of the lake. A hand minus an arm, and a body."

It was like I hit her in the face with a cold, wet carp. She fell back a half step and brought her hand up to her forehead. Her eyes narrowed like a cat about to pounce on a baby bunny. Then, just as quickly she regained her composure, ran her fingers through her hair and stared me in the eye.

"I have no idea of what you're talking about, Ms. Hughes," she repeated. "Can I help you find a coat? Our prices are the lowest in town."

Two things were clear: I had hit some kind of chord when I hinted at an errant body part in the lake, and she wasn't going to say another word to me about Mr. Yudeshenka.

I thanked her for her time and hustled myself out of there before one of the creatures bit me.

About an inch of snow had fallen, and the sidewalk was a bit slippery as I fiddled with my car keys. I had one foot in the driver's side of the car when a hand pushed down on my left shoulder, forcing me into the bucket seat. I grabbed the roof of the car trying to steady myself as Katya forced her face into mine. The rancid smell of cigarette breath poisoned the air between us

"Leave Yuri be," she said,

She slammed the car door on the tips of my fingers, then marched back into the store without looking back.

"Shit," I shouted, pulling my digits through the rubber tubing that insulates my car.

Please, God, don't let them be broken, I thought as I sucked on my left fore and middle fingers. Writing, taking care of my girls, just tying my shoes would all be seriously hampered if I couldn't use all my fingers. I would be *so* screwed

I turned on the engine and let the car warm up as I tentatively pulled my fingers from my mouth. Good thing I don't have time for manicures or even long fingernails, because both would probably have been wrecked. I gave both fingers a little wiggle. They seemed to work okay, but bruises were already beginning to form under the nails.

All right, Katya, message received, I thought as I drove back to the newsroom.

Chapter 8

There are parts about newspapering that I really love, like the constant interactions with a kaleidoscope of people. It keeps my faith in humanity alive. I've seen parents pray for the murderers of their children. I've seen generosity triumph over greed. I've interviewed Good Samaritans who eschewed the title of hero. The really cool part is watching history, up close and personal, and then writing about it. Even if it's nothing more than literature on the run, it's fun.

There are also parts I truly hate, such as having to hang around outside a court room or police station, like a jackal in a pack, waiting to ambush somebody. I hate calling parents whose children have just died, or been arrested or run away. I hate leaving messages on the phones of people I know will never call me back. But most of all, I really hate when sources lie to me. Had somebody lied to me? I wondered. Katya? Amber's grandma? And why hadn't Pace's boss returned my call?

I headed back toward downtown across the Washington Avenue Bridge until I came to Fourth Street South. A quick left took me into the underground parking garage of the Grain Exchange Building, which houses the newspaper. The smell of exhaust hung in the cold, damp air. Snow mixed with ice and road dirt, the stuff that melted off the cars' wheel wells, was stacked around like piles of elephant dung.

Fortunately, January, when it's common for temperatures to get into double-digits below zero, was behind us for this year. Gone was the need to plug the car into a heater that kept the oil in the oil pan warm and liquid enough for the car to start. Stuffing my hat and gloves in the pockets of my jacket, I made for the elevator that took me to the newsroom.

I tromped over to the desk I'd been assigned with the new beat and plopped down in the little blue swivel chair on wheels. Kicking off my Uggs, I gave my toes a little wiggle. Warm heavy boots that fend off the effects of the melting snow are one of the necessities of survival in Minnesota, but it sure feels good when you take them off.

"How's it going, guys?" I asked the two fellows who sat cheek-by-jowl at desks with chairs and computers identical to mine. One looked up and gave me half a salute with his right hand. The other mumbled "fine" from behind the newspaper he was reading.

I've been getting the impression my colleagues aren't especially happy to have me on their team. One of them, Slick Svenstad, has been a police reporter for as long as there have been cops, it seems. He sleeps with a police scanner next to his to bed, his wife told me after she had had too much to drink at the company Christmas party one year. He always has two cell phones and a pager attached to his belt. If one of his buddies at the station has a tip, he's reachable, 24/7/365—or 366 in a leap year.

His proudest moment came during the 1980s when he happened upon a bank robbery one noon. As bullets flew over his head, he ducked down behind a car and called the newsroom to dictate a minute-by-minute story about the carnage right before his very eyes. Unfortunately, this was well before the newspaper had even heard of the Internet and his words didn't reach his readers until the next morning, and by then the TV stations had already recapped the robbery for the ten o'clock news, making his story look like a rehash. Slick was the guy who gave me the little salute.

The other guy, Dick Richards, is even older than Slick. A card-carrying member of the National Rifle Association, he has been known to "pack heat," as he calls it, when he expects to work late. No hooligan is going to mug him as he walks to his car in the darkest of night without taking a bullet for his trouble, he has told me too many times. I have no idea what kind of gun he carries, and I don't care. I refuse to leave the building with him because I don't want to get caught in his friendly fire.

The day Thom put out a newsroom-wide email saying I would be the new missing persons reporter, Slick and Dick each called me and delivered the same message: Congratulations, but a missing persons beat is a stupid idea, they said.

"What's next? A reporter covering runaway dogs and cats caught in trees," Dick grumbled. "No offense, but this 'missing' thing is probably a good job for a girl."

"Now that sounds like you're disparaging women," Slick said. "Not me. I have the greatest respect for women. One of them wanted to be president, you know."

I looked at them both. What a pair they are. Slick is tall with white skin that makes his nicotine-stained teeth look dark as the cigar he smokes every day an hour before deadline, in the parking lot. He always wears a tie, a long-sleeved shirt and dress pants. He must have thin genes because his diet wouldn't account for his svelte, muscular physique.

Dick is about a foot shorter than Slick. The hair that remains on his head is dark and curly. I imagine he was once swarthy and trim, but now his skin is mottled, a paunch hangs over his belt and his man-boobs are bigger than mine. A couple of long, gray hairs poke through his bushy eyebrows. If someone had the wisdom to give him a trimmer for his nose hairs, he hasn't used it. Together, they sometimes remind me of The Joker and The Penguin.

Believe it or not, I actually like these guys, who finish each other's sentences, because I know exactly what they're thinking. They're dead wrong, but there's no subterfuge with them. No subtle bias against anyone. They're openly biased against everyone who is different from them. Just a couple of over-the-hill white guys who long for the days when they could call the newsroom and say, "Hey, Sweetheart, get me rewrite." I have no trouble imagining what they think about working for a gay man.

Regardless of their opinions, or perhaps because of them, these guys are good police reporters who are tight with the cops. That comes from years of doing favors—such as "losing" information about one of the blue brotherhood caught drinking on the job, or giving an officer a heads-up when a competing TV reporter is sniffing around an incident the cops would rather not see on the public airwaves.

In exchange, a few cops have been known to leave an investigative report where Dick might find it, or help Slick make a connection about a crime that may not otherwise be obvious. The point is, police reporting is a constant negotiation that would put the very best politician to the test.

Before Thom named me to this job, he told me the toughest part would be dealing with the guys. He was right. And wrong.

"So I hear you've found a missing hand," Dick said, folding his paper into quarters to tuck it under his arm while standing up. "Now there's a start on a tough week."

"Yeah, next thing you know you'll have a hand job," Slick laughed. So did Dick.

"Pardon me, but I must go take care of my daily duties," Dick said, heading toward the men's room.

"So how does your hubby appreciate your new gig?" Slick asked after Dick was gone.

"He's fine with it. Why?"

"He didn't tell you to quit the newspaper after you got his car firebombed on your last story?" he said.

"It was my car, not his. And Michael knows better than to tell me to do anything, especially when it comes to my job," I snapped.

Slick stuck his head back in his computer, like a turtle hiding from danger, rather than pursue the matter any further.

My husband, Michael Marks, is a business reporter for the St. Paul Post, archrival to the Minneapolis newspaper. It feels a bit odd, being married to the competition, but it's not unusual. So far, the Twin Cities is one of the few two-newspaper towns left in America. Couples who meet and marry, or at least cohabitate, at a newspaper are drawn to this market, because the odds of them both getting a job in the business are a little better here than most places.

Business reporters spend most of their time slogging through market reports and balance sheets. Reporters in search of the missing tend to hang out on the street, in coffee shops or with cops. That's just fine with me. We've never had to compete over a story, and I'd just as soon keep it that way. Our paths seldom cross on the job. Or, recently, at home. Michael moved out last month.

Although they apparently still worked, the fingers on my left hand throbbed as I gripped the steering wheel to drive home. But the pain was nothing compared to what I felt that horrible day last week when Michael told me he was leaving. I kept playing the moment over and over again in my head, like a bad movie.

Chapter 9

My emotions are still raw as I think back on that afternoon just a couple weeks ago. I'd had the week from hell and I was trying to grab an extra hour of sleep before the girls got home from school. The light in our bedroom was dim as the January sun was starting to drop. I had struggled against the sheets—fighting through terrifying nightmares of explosions and guys with their brains spilled all over the ground—and woke in a tangled mess. Michael was standing next to our bed. I sensed his presence before I opened my sleep-encrusted eyes to see him. I had snuck a cigarette before going to bed and instinctively put my hand to my mouth. I didn't want him to smell my awful breath. He didn't approve of my smoking, and I had been trying hard to quit. I didn't want him to know I had stumbled.

I sat up and swung my feet to the floor, perching on the side of the bed. The scarred oak floor was cold. The lettering on my long nightshirt proclaimed "Will write for food."

"Hi," I said, giving my hair a finger comb.

"What are you doing here?" He looked startled.

"What are you doing home in the middle of the day," I said as I grabbed my ratty red terrycloth bathrobe from the floor.

"I'm here to pack," he said.

"You off on assignment somewhere?"

"You can think that if you want to," he said.

"What does that mean?" I asked.

"I'm leaving. You."

"What?"

"I'm leaving you," he said again.

"Why?"

"Because I don't love you. I don't think I ever did," he said. He went to the kitchen, grabbed a beer from the fridge, popped the cap and chugged half the bottle.

I felt like I had been kicked in the head and gut at the same time by a huge horse. I thought we had an okay marriage. Two happy, healthy daughters. We owned a duplex, living on the first floor and renting out the second, in a neighborhood we loved. When we weren't working or parenting we read good books, watched good movies. We'd even gone to the Guthrie Theater together once or twice, although I couldn't tell you exactly when. We didn't have a dog, or even a cat. That shouldn't have mattered.

Looking back, I shouldn't have been surprised. For the past year, he always seemed to be working late, or out of town. Most of our communication was by voicemail or texting, always about our daughters, nothing more. That was the first time I had laid eyes on him in a week.

Journalism couplehood is complicated. Each has to figure out how to be competitors during the workday, then sleep together in the same bed at night. That means we can't talk about specifics on our stories. A few years ago a source wanted to fax some information to Michael at home. Our machine was complicated and Michael didn't know how to turn it on, but I did. He asked me to set the machine to take the fax, then leave the room. We built a brick wall between our work worlds. I wondered whether that professional separateness had bled into our stressful marriage.

I pushed past him and stumbled into the kitchen, where I put a pot of water on to boil and ground up three heaping teaspoons of Dunkin' Donuts whole bean coffee and poured them into the French press. Then I found my purse in the living room and dug out my cigarettes, lit up, and headed back for the kitchen. While the water came to a boil, I set my cigarette on the edge of the sink and leaned over to splash cold water on my face. I took a long, deep drag, filling my lungs with sweet nicotine. I closed my eyes to better smell the aroma and for a brief second I was back in my childhood, inhaling my father's musky scent, a mixture of coffee and cigarettes. The whistle of the teakettle jumpstarted my heart and I turned to him.

"I don't believe you," I said.

I could tell by the expression on his face he hadn't expected that reaction.

"Believe it," he said. "I'm leaving."

"I believe you're leaving," I said. "But I don't believe you don't love me. I don't believe you never loved me. "

I looked around our kitchen, the heart of our home. The butcher-block counter tops where we chopped garlic, onions and peppers were stained with their juice. I noticed the red stain from the night we left a glass of cabernet sauvignon next to the microwave. A basket of brown bananas, beginning to draw tiny flies, hung in the corner. I wondered if I could convince Rebecca to make banana bread. Michael, the girls and I had laughed and cried at various times in this room. It's where we had built our family. And now that family was threatened by whatever was really bothering him.

"It will be hard, but the girls will get it eventually," he said. "They'll love me more if I'm happy."

I took that to mean there was a lot more going on than his sudden dislike for me. Two years ago, under less pressure, he'd have known it's not the job of children to make their father happy. He'd have known it's his job as a father to make his daughters feel secure and loved. That's what I told him, calmly.

I could tell it wasn't what he had expected. His face and body language said he thought I would burst into tears, scream, and threaten a custody battle. That's exactly what I wanted to do. But somehow, by the goddess who watches over me, I didn't.

His reaction? He got mean, then landed another sucker punch.

"You're not the woman I married. I don't know who you are, but you're somebody I don't even like."

He delivered this line looking me straight in the eye, then he glanced away. I couldn't remember the last time he'd made eye contact with me.

I looked at his face closely, for the first time in a long time. Why hadn't I noticed the strain in his eyes before, the purse of his lips? Suddenly he was a little wan, a little grayer, a lot older. How had I missed those signs? Because the girls and my work, which are the other two legs of the three-legged stool that was my life, had consumed all my energy? Had I let the part that was Michael go unattended for too long? Probably.

"I believe you need a break," I said. "Take it. Give yourself all the space you need. Live somewhere else for a while. There are many ways to be married. But I deny that you never loved me, that you don't love me now. And I will not allow you to destroy this family."

Chapter 10

To keep the girls and their father on good terms, we decided to have dinner together as often as he wanted. Tonight was the night. I pushed through boots, ice skates and fallen backpacks in our mudroom and stumbled into my kitchen greeted by the garlicky smell of spaghetti sauce simmering on the stove.

Rebecca stirred the sauce with a wooden spoon in one hand and held the TV remote in the other, flipping through channels. For some reason she seemed undecided between MTV and a cable poker game.

"Hey," she said, without looking away from the TV as I walked in. "Dad said he'd be here in fifteen. Dinner's in twenty. Suzy's in her room, knitting, I think."

"Hi, Sweetie," I said giving her a hug.

I stuck my head into Suzy's room. "Hi, Mom," she said without looking up, her short, fat knitting needles clicking so fast they sounded like wheels on a train track. "How was your day?"

"Fine. Busy. How was school?"

"The same. When's dinner?"

"Rebecca says about twenty minutes, so why don't you finish up there and go wash your hands?"

I went into the bedroom to change out of my black slacks, sweater and boots. I like black. In fact, my entire closet is full of black everything. I even wear black scarves. It could be a fashion statement, but really, it's a matter of practicality. I never have to worry about whether my clothes match when I get dressed in the dark. It cuts way down on the time I have to spend shopping. It's also slimming.

But apparently not slimming enough. While I was wrestling with the zipper on my jeans—black, of course—a minute later I heard Michael walk in the door, say hi to the girls and pull the chair from the round wooden table that was my grandmother's. When I stepped into the kitchen, I saw that he was still in his work "uniform"—khaki Dockers, a denim shirt and a ragged navy tie.

Rebecca was quiet about her day but Suzy chatted on about the chick hatching from its egg in her classroom. Then Michael talked about the latest reporter to leave the newsroom for a job in public relations.

"He's the third experienced reporter to leave this month."

"Are they going to replace him?" Suzy asked.

"Doubt it," Michael replied. "But if they do it will be with somebody much younger, and cheaper. "

Dinner gone, I told the girls to get to their homework. As I scraped the table scraps into the bag we keep for neighborhood compost, Michael shrugged into his Columbia down jacket.

"Should we talk about us, Michael?" I asked. "I can make an appointment with a counselor."

"I'm not ready for that, " he said.

I shivered in the wall of icy air that rushed into the warm kitchen when he opened the back door to leave.

Chapter 11

FEBRUARY 13

Thom likes to have a quick chat with each of his reporters before he goes into the morning meeting, where he and the other editors talk about what they expect to see that day. Apparently it was my turn, because I looked up to see him standing at my desk.

"Whatta ya got for me, Hughes?" he wanted to know. "Tell me I'll have something to offer from you."

"I don't expect I'll have a story for you today," I said. Instead, I filled him in on my conversations with Amber's grandma and Yuri's wife.

"Katya said they were fighting over the animals. That's what they call the furs."

"Are you sure she meant dead furs?" Thom asked.

That's what she said, but, thinking back, I realized there was an odd look in her eye when she made the comment. At first I had thought she was talking about pets, of the cat and dog variety.

"Where did she say her husband was living?" Thom asked.

"Moose Meadow."

"Didn't we have a story a while back about people keeping exotic animals, like lions and tigers, out there? Maybe she meant something bigger than Petunia the Pussycat," he said, over his shoulder as he moved on to the next reporter.

Hmm, I thought. Maybe she did. I punched "exotic animals" into our database and 16 stories from the past five years popped up. Were the counties outside the Twin Cities overrun with roving packs of wildlife? In the past few years law enforcement had raided half a dozen farms, taking away leopards, tigers, lions, cougars, mixed-breed big cats, camels and black bears. Most of the felons were convicted on federal charges for selling the animals or killing them for their hides, or transporting the hides and animals across state lines.

Why would anybody want to keep those kinds of animals around? I wondered.

I placed a call to a county sheriff I had known in Rochester who moved to Wright County, where most of the activity was. He picked up on the first ring.

"Business must be slow in Moose Meadow, Minnesota," I said.

"This must be that wise-ass reporter, Skeeter, who moved from Rochester to the big bad city," he replied.

"How did you know it's me?"

"Even out here in Wright County we have caller ID," he said. "What can I do for you, Skeeter?"

"I'm harboring an idle curiosity about exotic animals," I said. "Got time for a few questions?"

"You're not going to quote me, now are you?" he asked. "The feds took over that operation a long time ago and you know how they can be about their territory."

"Nope. I'm just wondering a few things. Like, why would anybody want to own an exotic animal?"

"I've asked that question myself," he said. "I think it's a macho thing."

"Meaning?"

"Meaning these guys are bullies and having big animals makes them feel like real men," he said.

"So they're compensating for something, or a lack of something?" I asked.

"Yeah," he chuckled. "Compensating."

"What are these guys usually like?"

"Is this going to be long?" he asked. "I've got a report due in five minutes."

"I have quite a few more questions."

"Look, I like you, Skeeter, and it's been a long time since we got together. Why don't you come out here? I'll buy you a cup of coffee and we can have a real conversation."

As the sheriff spoke I watched Dick returning from his ablutions, for today. When he reached his desk he took the quarter-folded newspaper from under his arm and laid it down next to a box of donuts someone from the night crew had apparently left behind. He reached in the box and grabbed a jelly donut, taking a big bite until its contents squished out the sides and dropped on his shirt. I prayed he had washed his hands before he left the restroom.

"I'll be there in 45 minutes," I told my friend. "I want to talk about lions and tigers."

As I rang off, Dick cranked his head around his computer, wiping jelly from the corner of his mouth with his finger.

"Did I hear you say tigers?" he asked.

I explained that I was talking with someone in Wright County.

"I live out there, you know," he said, a detail I had forgotten. "The place has been overrun with all these goddamn communists."

"What do you mean, 'communists'?" I asked.

"You know, the Russkies. When the wind picks up in the evening you can hear their god-awful Russian music playing."

Although I usually only half listen to him, this time I paid attention.

"And there's noise coming from their place all night," he said. "It's worse than Delta flying their jets the whole time."

"How long have you lived in Moose Meadow?" I asked Dick.

"Missus and I planted our flag there about thirty years ago, well before it got so citified," he replied. "We paid off the mortgage ten years ago."

They had 17 acres, then sold seven to his son-in-law a few years ago. "Myrna likes having the grandkids nearby."

"How close is your place to the 'Russkies'?" I couldn't believe he used that term.

"They're on the land behind mine," he said, then pulled his head back in front of his computer screen. The conversation was over.

I gave Thom a quick finger wave on my way out the door and minutes later I was heading west on Highway 55. It was one of those days when the sun is bright, the sky is blue and the temperature hovered around not-too-cold, maybe 25 degrees. I had the top down on my little red convertible and the heat jacked way up. The fresh air helped clear away the Dick-ick. Ewww.

When Dick moved here Highway 55 shot through farmland, but now it's lined with a depressing series of strip malls punctuated too often with stoplights. For about ten miles on the two-lane highway I followed a black SUV that bore a bumper sticker proclaiming: "Driver does not brake for protesters or celebrities." It was slow going. Fortunately, Minnesota Public Radio was airing a report about the aftereffects of the nuclear meltdown at Chernobyl, so I had something to occupy my thoughts. As I sat at one of the traffic lights, a very long train of boxcars rumbled along the railroad line that runs parallel to Highway 55. Dick had complained about noise at night. I wondered if what he heard was a train.

Finally, I pulled off the highway and followed a sign pointing to downtown Moose Meadow. The road led to Moose Lake, where about thirty fishing houses stuck from the ice like whiskers on an old man's chin. I hung a left and made my way to the county sheriff's office. The deputy was standing at the front desk in the modern, cinderblock building, handing in what looked to be the report he'd mentioned on the phone.

"Hi Skeeter," he said. "Let's go into my office. Still drink your coffee black?"

We stopped in a small room where he poured us each coffee in small white Styrofoam cups, then I followed him down a tiled hall to a room big enough for his desk, a phone and a visitor's chair.

"So you were asking about lions and tigers and bears, oh my?" he said with a laugh.

"Yes. Tell me about the people who keep exotic animals." I pulled out my notebook, the long, skinny one with the wire looped through the top.

"They're mysterious," he said.

"Meaning they're hidden?"

"Yes, that, and they like to drop hints to neighbors that they may be involved in terrorism."

"Are they terrorists?"

"Nobody knows for sure because they mostly stay to themselves."

"I guess they'd have pretty big properties," I said.

"Often they have big chunks of land, yes," he replied. "Maybe ten acres."

"Is there serious money in exotic animals?"

He leaned back in his chair and laced his fingers behind his head. I remembered that he always seemed to like talking to the press.

"Some. I wouldn't call it big. The animals probably sell for $5,000 to $10,000, but these guys usually have other money-making operations going on."

"Such as?"

"Illegal weapons. Drugs. Or both. Sometimes they'll swap the animals for stolen fancy foreign cars."

"How do they feed these animals?" I asked. "I don't suppose they'd just go to Costco every day and buy a lot of meat."

As I asked the question another deputy stuck his head in the office. "Hey, looks like you're a media star again there, Rob."

"No, we're just chatting. This reporter wants to know how folks feed the exotic animals."

"Kids sell 'em roadkill," the other deputy said. "Sometimes the neighbor's dogs disappear. Come see me when you're done, Rob."

I looked up at him and for a moment all I could think of was Michael. Don't know why. Maybe it was the tilt of his head, the way his hair fell. My mind spun away from the interview. What was going to happen to us, I wondered. Would we be able to survive this patch of bumpy road? Was it just a patch of bumpy road, or the end of a cul-de-sac? Would I be a single mom juggling too much? And what exactly was going on with him? I didn't know the answer to that question. Oh my God, I thought. The Michael situation was pushing me off my game professionally. This had to stop. I pulled my focus back just in time to hear Rob say "… have been suspicions for years that these guys poach deer, then feed them to their animals."

"Isn't all that illegal?" I asked.

"Yes, it is," he said.

He noted that the community is changing. People, like Dick, bought in Moose Meadow years ago because they wanted their privacy. Don't ask, don't tell about anything your neighbor may be doing, was the rule.

"With properties that big neighbors are far away from each other, so it's pretty easy to not know what's going on," he said.

"Isn't that changing?"

"Right again."

I remembered a news story from a few years ago that said more people who work in the city were buying homes in the far western suburbs because they thought they were getting away from the big-city problems.

"Is that why there have been so many busts in the past few years?"

"That's part of it, I'm sure," he replied. "These city folk bring their nosiness out here along with their fancy clothes and their Brie."

I thanked him for his time, then rose to leave. As I was standing at the door, another question occurred to me.

"Is there a general type who likes to own animals? Outdoorsy types? Animal lovers? "

"A lot of times they're foreign-born," he said. "Some say they're animal lovers, but I think that's just an excuse."

"Foreign born? From where?"

"Eastern Europe, mostly," the sheriff said. "Swarthy types."

"Is there a particular species they like?"

"I hear they're always looking for white tigers," he said.

"White tigers?" I asked. "Is there such a thing?"

"Beats me," he said. "That's just what I've heard."

He escorted me past the heavy, locked door and to the front reception desk, then headed back to his other meeting, I supposed. How many secrets did Moose Meadow harbor? I wondered, looking up to see the sky quickly filling with thickening clouds.

Chapter 12

It was well past lunchtime and my stomach was beginning to growl. Should I find a place to eat here, or try to make it back to the city before the snows began to fly? Might as well soak up a little Moose Meadow color, I figured. I put the roof up on my car and headed back into town. Two quick rights and there I was in front of Aunt Bea's Family Restaurant.

The storefront window was steamed from the heat inside, and the manager had turned on a dozen overhead fans, even though it was about twenty degrees outside. A server hid behind a white lattice barrier catching a smoke.

A moment after I slid into a booth, a waitress was at my side, black-and-brown–plastic coffee pot in hand.

"Can I warm you up?" She was too thin with short, frizzy hair and at least five tattoos I could see, including a rose on her neck and an interlocking chain on her right bicep. Below pierced brows, her eyes had a look that said she was working the second shift of a three-shift day, and it had been like that most of her short life. "The special is a salad, Swedish meatballs with creamed corn and apple pie for dessert."

"I'll take the special," I said. "Where's the restroom?"

I followed her directions and availed myself of the one-toilet room. As I washed my hands I took a good look at a poster placed next to the mirror with the picture of a woman who wore a black eye and a broken tooth. "Getting hit is never OK," said the message, along with a phone number for a local women's shelter. Apparently folks who moved here from Minneapolis didn't leave all their troubles behind.

A brown plastic bowl with iceberg lettuce, a few croutons and heavy blue cheese dressing in a little white paper cup on the side waited for me when I returned to the booth. Music from a country western radio station played softly in the background. As I nibbled I inspected the ten-foot-long blue marlin that hung on the wall, and another fish I couldn't name opposite it.

"More coffee?" my waitress asked.

"Sure," I said. "Are those fish real?"

"They are," she said. "The owner caught them. I thought one was male and the other female, but it turns out one is a subspecies of the other." This is a lady who knows her fish, I thought.

As she poured my coffee I noticed that she wore a button that pictured a little boy with his arm around what appeared to be a tiger cub. "Who's the cutie on your button?" I asked.

"That's my little boy," she said with a smile.

"Is that a tiger cub with him in the picture?"

"It sure is," she said, pulling the pin out from her shirt a bit so she could take another look at it. "We just love animals."

"Who took the picture?"

"A photographer who has a studio just off Highway 55," she said.

I asked her where the photographer got the tiger.

"I think he got it from one of those guys sitting over there in the corner," she said with just a slight nod of her head.

I tried not to be too obvious as I took a gander at three men who sat at a round table in the back of the restaurant. They all appeared to be in their fifties. Two of them had the exact same bald pattern, so I guessed they were brothers about five years apart. The brothers were both barrel-chested. One had a beard, the other a mustache. The third man didn't look related to the other two, who were talking intently.

"Folks say they've got wild animals on their land," she whispered to me conspiratorially. "The other waitress and I think that's just terrible."

"Why?" I asked.

"It's just not right," she said. "Lions and tigers belong in the jungle."

"Then why did you get a picture taken of your son with a tiger?"

"They're fine when they're just cubs," she said. "But once they're grown they belong in the jungle."

I wasn't going to argue the illogic of that one. Instead, I asked her if she knew where those guys in the corner lived. I thought I'd just go take a little look-see.

"Out Highway 55 about a mile and a half," she said. In small towns, everyone knows where everyone lives, even the most mysterious. "If you turn off Dorset Road and go another two miles you'll see their fence. But be careful if you go there."

"Why?" I asked again.

"My brother-in-law's farm is near there," she said. "He has a flock of sheep. Every so often one or two go missing. He thinks these guys are stealing his sheep to feed their tigers."

After I finished my pie—those cotton underpants from Target felt even tighter—my waitress brought the check.

"Why are you asking about the cats?" she wanted to know. From the corner of my eye I saw the other waitress pour coffee for another table while cocking her head so she could overhear our conversation.

"I'm a reporter for the *Citizen*," I told her, pulling a card from my purse. "I'm kinda looking into the big cat thing." "I hope you put an article in the paper about how people treat these animals," she said very quietly, slipping the card into the pocket of her black jeans. Then, a little louder, she added, "Have a nice day."

I left her a thirty percent tip, and made sure she saw me stuff five dollars into the jar by the cash register. It sported a sign: "Just a little loose change will help a homeless animal's life."

Does that include tigers, I wondered.

Chapter 13

Because it's small and the hard top fits on airtight, my del Sol heats up quickly. This was especially good today because the temperature was dropping fast as I got back on Highway 55. I turned off just after the Target parking lot, then passed a firing range as I headed down a dirt road that hadn't been plowed in a while. The undercarriage of my low-riding car scraped a layer off the snow that remained between the ruts created by the tires of heavy equipment. The flat farmland, broken only by the occasional fence, felt like Somewhere, South Dakota, even though I was only 45 minutes from the Twin Cities.

Driving along I watched for the telltale signs the deputy mentioned: outbuildings mostly hidden by trees. Unfortunately, almost every property had those features. Was everybody harboring tigers?

I had gone about three miles when I looked in my rearview mirror and saw I was being followed by a silver blue sports car that rode even lower to the ground than my car. On closer inspection, I realized the driver was one of the three men who had been eating at Aunt Bea's. He was traveling at a pretty good clip, so I sped up. Didn't want him on my tail. After about a mile he turned to the left and I kept going until I couldn't see his car any more. Then I turned around and headed back.

When I got to where he had turned off I slowed down. A quarter-mile further down the road I noticed a fence camouflaged with brush. I pulled over and studied the scene.

It looked like a farmhouse from the early 1900s. Its paint had long since peeled away and the roof sagged a little further on the left than the right. It was one-and-a-half stories high, tucked in a depression in the ground. A windmill several feet behind the house spun at top speed, pushed by winds coming in fast from the west, indicating a change in the weather. About 100 feet away to the left a shiny new corrugated metal building surrounded by a new chain-link fence loomed. A beat-up Ford truck froze just outside the fence. The silver blue car sat in front in stark contrast to the rest of the place.

Glad I had worn my Sorel boots instead of the Uggs, I got out of the car and sunk into calf-deep snow as I trudged through a ditch between the road and the farm fence, which was a couple of strands of wire attached to metal posts. The original fence likely collapsed long ago and the current owners, who apparently weren't very good at building fences, wanted to clearly mark the property line. It was easy to step over the wire but hard to make my way in deep snow to a copse of scraggly bushes. I pretended not to see the half dozen "no trespassing" signs.

I kept one eye on the house while I crept closer to the outbuilding. The scent of snow hung heavy in the air, along with something I couldn't quite identify. Paint? No, not that acidic. It had more of a musky smell. Rotting wood? Maybe. Rotting meat? I hoped not. As I scanned the yard I saw something off in one corner. It was dirty brown.

I was two steps away from my camouflage when I heard pop... pop. Pop...Pop. Pop. I froze at the sound of gunshots. Gunshots had come close, too close, while I was working another story last month and I didn't like it. Was someone shooting at me? I hadn't seen any bullets hit the snow or the trees nearby. I don't like guns and I don't want to get shot. The voice of a normal person in my head said, run. Run as fast as you can. Jump in your car and get out of here. Over the years. I've learned to ignore that voice. One day that might be a critical mistake. Was today the day?

A moment later there was another pop, pop. This time I realized the sound came from a distance. Probably the firing range, I figured. Even so, the sound, combined with adrenaline and the caffeine in my bloodstream, made my heart pound faster. I prayed the shooter's aim was good enough that an errant bullet didn't come my way.

Tossing a quick glance toward the house, I continued to creep through a foot of snow to get a better look at the brown gunk just this side of the outbuilding. From about twelve feet away, I was close enough to see what it was: half a sheep. The back half. Bloody paw prints twice the size of my hands had smeared the snow. I'm a city girl, not a tracker. I couldn't tell how many animals might have made the marks. Maybe one. Maybe more. But given that half the sheep remained I guessed that the predator was either sated, or saving a snack for later. I didn't want to watch the second course.

The bolts that held the building together fit imperfectly, which created peep holes. After throwing another look at the house to make sure no one was watching me, I made my way closer to the building. The snow muffled the sound of my steps.

With my eye right up to the hole in the metal, I spied inside. It was a big building, maybe the size of half a football field, with a dirt floor. My brothers, who knew every car ever made, would have loved to get inside to scope out all the cool cars. I tried to recall the name of the car with doors that open like wings. DeLuca? DeLorean? What I guessed was a Maserati was parked at one end, next to a vintage motorcycle. Off to the right were several wooden boxes about eight feet long, and behind that, video equipment. Off to the left was a square cage maybe eight feet by eight feet. A white tiger was sleeping in the corner. Was this the elusive white tiger the sheriff had told me about? And what was it doing in a shed in Moose Meadow, Minnesota? It looked so gentle I almost wanted to whisper "here, kitty, kitty" and scratch its ears.

I figured I was pressing my luck just being there and it was time to hightail it. But first I thought I'd get a better look at the pickup truck parked out front. When I got back to the office I could run a check on the license plate and at least figure out the name and address of the owner. I scooted around the building, then over to the truck, where I peeked in the window to see if maybe there was a hint of what was going on inside. A videocassette, bearing white tape covered with blood, rested on the passenger seat.

I was suddenly faced with two oddities. One, a videocassette is dated technology. Whoever these guys were they were seriously behind the times. But then, again, in some ways, I am too. We still have a video player at home that works.

Second, and more important, theft is clearly a violation of journalistic ethics. I knew I shouldn't take it. But what if it were evidence of some heinous crime? What if it were footage of someone's death? Didn't I have a duty to at least examine it? The blood smears tipped the scale for me.

The truck door opened with a loud squeak. I grabbed the tape and gave the door a quick hip check. When it squealed again, I looked up to see a curtain pushed aside in a window in the house. Now it was time to make my own tracks.

I ran as fast as I could in my Sorels and dove back into the stand of trees just as a man came to the back door of the house, a shotgun in his hands. He stepped out onto a back porch and stood for a while, like an animal sniffing in the air.

Chapter 14

I prayed he wouldn't hear my pounding heart. After a while he seemed satisfied that there was no threat and went back in the house. I waited another ten minutes trying to figure out who the guy with the shotgun was. He sure wasn't one of the barrel-chested brothers. In fact, he was svelte, wearing what looked like the pants to a pinstripe suit, and a white shirt with the sleeves rolled up. He was clean-shaven and had sable-black hair. His movements were smooth, without any wasted motion, like a panther. Nice ass, I couldn't help but notice. Who was this guy? I made my way to my car carefully. Thank God the snow muffled sound so well, I thought. I was turning left on Highway 55, just past the Target parking lot, when my heart finally started to return to a normal rhythm.

Snowflakes falling in clumps slowed traffic back to the cities, so it was early evening and dark when I pulled into our garage. Michael's 1999 Mazda was in its spot and I saw the light burning in our kitchen as I gave the rope on the garage door a good yank. I wondered what he was doing here again.

Michael and the girls were sitting around the dinner table, dishes still dirty from the remains of spaghetti. Third night in a row for spaghetti, but no one seemed to mind. A fourth setting held a place at the table for me. Suzy was regaling them with a story about a kid at school who had stuffed his entire fist down his throat, then got it stuck, while I picked up the plate and looked in the saucepot. Dried bits of tomato stuck to the sides. I shrugged and looked over to the colander, where someone had drained the spaghetti noodles. They were dry on top, but I a took a fork full and slathered a gob of butter on top, then sprinkled some Parmesan cheese from the green foil can on top of that.

"Al dente," I said as I slid into my spot at the table.

"Another night for spaghetti," was Michael's greeting to me.

"You could have made something different," was my reply.

The girls looked at each other, picked up their plates and left the table.

"Why are you here?" I asked Michael between mouthfuls.

"The girls were worried when you were late. They called me. Skeeter, this has got to stop."

"This? What's 'this'?" I asked.

"'This' is your failure to accept your responsibilities to the girls," he said.

"My responsibilities? What about yours? You're the one who moved out."

"The girls know they can reach me any time. Can they say the same about you? Rebecca said she called you five times and each time your phone rolled over to your answering system. She was terrified you'd landed in a pile of snow again."

"My phone was in my purse. I didn't hear it ring."

"A likely excuse."

"It's not an excuse. It's what happened. I have a job just like you do, Michael. "

"And exactly where were you on your job today?"

I gave him a quick summary, starting with Dick's comment about the "Russkies" and finishing with the white tiger in the metal outbuilding. I didn't mention the videotape, which I had stuck in my purse before I entered the house.

"I can't say I'm surprised you would do something so stupid," he said with a sigh as he rose from the table. "You always were the dumpster diver."

As a business reporter, Michael does most of his work with documents he downloads or gets from public filings. Seldom does he actually get dirty. I, on the other hand, have been known to actually crawl into heating vents, or even dumpsters if necessary, to get information. It irritates me when Michael, Mr. I'm-above-such-shenanigans, calls me a dumpster diver. And he knows it.

"And you were always the manipulator," I snapped. "Now Rebecca is learning the same trick."

"What's that mean?" he asked.

"It means she's playing us and taking your side when she calls you saying she can't reach me," I said. "If she needed something she could have just called you in the first place. We are still both parents to both girls, aren't we?"

The tick-tock on the kitchen clock reverberated between us a full thirty seconds before either of us spoke.

"We weren't going to bring the girls into this," Michael said through clenched teeth.

No, we weren't, I thought.

"If we're going to work this out like adults, we have to point the girls away from us. It's classic daughter behavior to side with the father in this kind of situation."

"Now you're a shrink as well as a dumpster diver," he said.

Yeah, I was the dumpster diver in our relationship, back when our relationship worked. I thought about that time before kids when we spent hours imagining our future. We didn't believe the malcontents who said newspapers would die from lack of interest. Instead, we saw ourselves growing into better jobs, maybe to bigger papers in bigger towns. We'd have two children, a nice but not extravagant house in the city, maybe a dog. We'd make the decisions together. We'd have each other. Us against the world.

So here we are. We have two wonderful daughters, a middle class house in the middle of the city. The jobs we've got are good, although neither of us knows how long they will last. Journalism positions—particularly in print—are disappearing three times as fast as in other occupations. Still, we're both committing journalism on a regular basis, and it feels right.

Then I thought about exactly what Michael had said on that horrible day. "I'm leaving. You." Just like that. It was two separate thoughts. Thought one: leaving. Thought two: leaving me.

Terrible days and nights followed. I'd read murder stories and fantasized how I could do him in. Poisoning's painless, right? What about electrocution? Guns and knives are too messy. I'm not strong enough to strangle him, although it sure would feel good. Maybe I should throw him in Lake Harriet and while he's down there he can research my story, I thought.

"What happened, Michael?" I asked.

"I don't know," he said. "I only know I don't love you."

"Remember when we first moved in together," I said to him. "We had that crappy apartment in that lousy part of town and our furniture came from my mother's basement. Remember sitting on the living room floor making our dinner of peanut butter sandwiches with our one knife and eating it on a wooden box filled with old New Yorkers?"

"You made brownies for dessert," he said. "You burned 'em,"

"Because we didn't have a timer."

"You cried."

"Because I'd wasted a brownie mix and an egg."

"That was stupid," he said.

"I remember your arms around me like steel, the smell of your sweater, the pressure in my chest when you consoled me."

"We made love in the kitchen," he said.

"Without curtains."

We both laughed at that. Then the kitchen went quiet. Again.

"I gotta go," he said.

I vomited the buttered noodles into the garbage disposal, then cleaned up the kitchen. Do daughters really side with their fathers in these situations? I didn't know, but it sounded likely. What was I doing here? I wondered. Was I sacrificing my marriage for my career? For my family? In the newsroom I'm made of titanium, but when it comes to fighting with my husband I'm all bluster. Maybe there was a reason Lois Lane never married. Yeah, I always was the dumpster diver.

Chapter 15

The girls had gone to bed but the adrenaline was still swishing through my veins from the afternoon's adventure. Trying to relax, I got on line and skimmed the evening's news. CNN, the *New York Times*, the *Los Angeles Times*, the competition in St. Paul.

I glanced at my purse, which I had dropped on the kitchen counter. I could see the corner of the videotape poking through the fake leather. What had I done? I stole the thing. I'd never stolen anything before this. What was happening to my judgment? Was the stress of my disintegrating marriage knocking my thinking askew in my professional life? A cheap shrink would say that I stole the tape because it gave me some small sense of control in my otherwise out-of-control life. So now what? I had the stolen tape. I couldn't take it back. I decided I might as well watch it.

It was eleven p.m. when I grabbed a beer from the fridge, then slipped the tape into the machine and settled into my overstuffed chair with the chocolate-colored chenille slipcover. With one hand I took a long pull on my beer and with the other fast-forwarded. The static continued so long I stopped the fast-forward and just let it play while I dragged my tired bones from my chair, cursing that I had swiped a blank tape. Squatting before our VCR, which we keep on a stand under the TV, I was just about to reach in and take the tape when a roar shook the living room, knocking me back on my butt and I spilled the beer. I hit the volume control right away so the sound wouldn't wake the girls, then moved back to my chair to watch more.

The scene was the inside of the building on the farm. The tiger had looked healthy when it was curled up in the corner, but the tape made clear it was underfed, and hungry. It lunged at the sheep, which tried to run around the small cage, bleating its little heart out. Sheep and tiger went around like that a couple of laps, until the tiger had the sheep trapped in the corner. Then, with one bold leap, it grabbed the sheep with its jaws on the front half and chomped down hard.

The three men I had seen in the restaurant were gathered around the chain metal cage where the tiger had been sleeping. Empty bottles of vodka and cigarette butts littered the floor and one of the barrel-chested brothers was crouched outside the cage with a wad of money in his hand. Another half dozen men I didn't recognize stood around hooting and hollering as a guy holding the money looked at a stopwatch. I guessed they were betting on how long it would take the tiger to devour the poor sheep.

While the tiger gnawed its dinner the brother holding the money turned to the other brother and said something. The men started to shout, clap and pound the floor as the younger brother worked the padlock on the tiger's cage, then crept in, grabbed the back half of the sheep and pulled it from the cage. The men gave a round of applause to the brother, who looked more afraid than heroic. Off to the side stood Mr. Pinstripe, quietly watching the show with a smile on his face that gave me a shiver. The tape ended.

It's been said that if you watch violence repeatedly you become inured to it. Didn't work for me. Each repeat was as repulsive as the last. I watched it a couple more times, trying to study the crowd. Then I saw him, standing alone in the corner of the shed looking a little sick. I couldn't be positive, but it looked like Yuri.

Chapter 16

I had planned to follow up on my three "missings" when I got to work in the morning, but Slick and Dick were both assigned to cover murders in a Wisconsin funeral home, so I was the fallback for daily cop reporting. I suspected I also got the fill-in job as a wrist slap for not coming up with anything better on the case of the hand in the lake. Whatever the reason, it meant trudging over to the cop house to read through the reports of the day before.

I dislike checking the daily record. It means reading highly detailed reports about gruesome crimes. The thirteen-year-old girl picked up by a biker gang and taken back to their house for multiple rape. The abuse of an eighty-one-year-old man by his son-in-law, who forced him to sit naked on a soapy plastic chair in the shower until his testicles slipped through the drainage holes in the chair and got stuck. The witness description of a kindergartener whose head split like a watermelon when the little boy was accidentally run over by his school bus. Plus suicides. Somebody has to read through this stuff and decide which reports the editors are likely to want to put in the newspaper. Most of the time they nix stuff that's too graphic, unless it's done in public or by a public person. But the images often stick in my mind like a bad movie. Sergeant Victoria Olson and I happened to cross paths while I was there.

"What's up with your buddies, Slick and Dick?" she asked.

"Meaning?"

"Meaning I've been hearing they're pretty tight with some of the old guard around here," she said.

"Tight? How tight?"

"Look-the-other-way-occasionally tight."

"To what end?" I asked.

"To get a bigger story," she said.

I didn't doubt it. Slick and Dick had been around for so long they probably had pictures of J. Edgar Hoover in drag. Well, I was new at this beat, but I could play the game as well as they could. At least that's what I told Sergeant Olson.

"I'll remember that," she said with a smile as she continued past the subway tile that lines the Minneapolis police station.

I trotted back to the newsroom with plans to write up a couple of short items for the public safety page. Before I could even plug in my password my phone rang.

"I'm so sorry I didn't return your call sooner," said Margaret Anderson, Pace Palmer's supervisor. "I've been out of town. Didn't have a minute to myself. You know how that goes, I'm sure. But I'm so glad you called. I'm worried sick about her. No one here has heard a word from her. That's just not like Pace."

"I see from the police report that Pace is thirty-six, tall and thin, but that doesn't tell me much. Can you fill in a little bit more about her?"

"Pace was—I mean, is—one of our most conscientious employees. She's been with us about two years."

It was common to see her in the office on weekends and well into the evening, Pace's boss said. "Before she came to work for us she was a pediatric nurse. When Pace learned she had multiple sclerosis she left nursing. Although she was only mildly impaired she feared one day she would drop a baby.

"I'm sure it was hard for her. She loved taking care of kids. She often said, 'Once a nurse, always a nurse.' She couldn't bear the thought of hurting a patient. We really value her around here because of that. She watched our product work and wanted to be part of the team."

"What does your company do?" I asked.

"We make the BabySavr. All one word, no 'E.' If you mention us in the newspaper, be sure to drop the 'E'. BabySavr is a device that can be inserted into the trachea of infants who have trouble breathing," she said, adding that it reduced the incidence of sudden infant death syndrome dramatically. Sounded like a miracle device to me, so I wanted to know how it worked, but she wouldn't tell me.

"Proprietary technology," she said. "I will tell you it uses a special material that stops the airways to the lungs from collapsing. We were founded 17 years ago by a professor at the University of Minnesota medical school."

"What's Pace's position?"

"She's research coordinator."

When I worked at the Rochester newspaper I briefly covered medical research. I remembered that in order to be approved by the U.S. Food and Drug Administration, a medical device has to be tested first on animals and then on humans. After years of testing in dogs and pigs, the inventor often forms a company and sends it to as many as thirty universities in the U.S. and particularly Western Europe. In this case, the researchers would likely be pediatricians with university appointments who specialize in baby breathing disorders. The whole process can take ten to twenty years.

"Would you explain Pace's job to me in detail?" I asked.

"Of course. As the universities that test our product do their work, they send their data to us. Pace's job is to keep track of all that data, then, when it's complete, help us analyze the results and submit our report to the FDA."

"But if you already have BabySavr on the market, why do you need someone like Pace to continue to analyze the data? I would think you already have that part complete."

"Good question. We have other products using the same proprietary technology under research now. Pace is working with the newest versions of our products." Ms. Anderson declined to discuss what those newest products might be. "Proprietary, you know."

As she spoke I took notes on the computer. We had been talking for a while; I was starting to get a cramp in my left hand. Wrist, elbow and hand ailments plague the newsroom. I pulled away from the computer for a moment, shook both hands in the air, then picked up a pen and a legal-sized tablet and began to doodle flowers with big round pedals and long leafy stems.

"Who are her friends at work?" I asked. "I'd like to talk to them."

"I'm probably her closest friend, even though I'm her boss."

"Were there any men or women in her life?"

"I think she was involved with a man for a long time, but that seemed to have ended. That was why she was taking this vacation. She said she needed to get away for a couple of weeks. She had plenty of time in the bank, so we all encouraged her to go, even though her work here is so important to what we do. It's tough covering for her, even temporarily."

"When was she supposed to leave?"

"August 4. She said she would email us while she was gone. I was surprised I didn't hear from her, but I figured she was having such a good time she didn't want to check in."

"When was she supposed to come back to work?"

"August 18."

Ms. Anderson said she called Pace's home and cell numbers and left messages. Then she stopped by her condo and knocked on the door. No one answered. "She lives in one of those apartment buildings that's been turned into condos near Lake Harriet. It's probably got seventy or eighty units. There weren't any newspapers piled up outside or anything. I didn't see any neighbors I could ask, either."

I knew the location. It's near where I had coffee with the hand fisher. "Did she have any family in the area who might be missing her?"

"Pace never mentioned any family." And she never told anyone at work her man's name, according to her boss. "I got the impression that he had a lot of money. I know he used to send her big bouquets of flowers at work. But I think he was jealous that she spent so much time in the office. She made some comment before she went on vacation that perhaps they would still be together if she had taken a little time with him earlier on."

I thanked her for her help, and left her with my phone numbers and email address in case she thought of something else I should know.

"Are you going to put an article in the paper about us?" she asked.

"I don't know," I replied in all honesty. So far I didn't have much to write about. Just a woman who didn't show up at work.

"If you want any more information about the company, you can check the St. Paul Post from a couple of weeks ago. They did a very flattering article on us."

I rang off, went to the competition's website and punched in "BabySavr." In a nanosecond an article appeared: "Shareholders breathing heavy as stock soars." Author: Michael Marks, my estranged husband.

I read Michael's article. Not bad. His prose has always been clean. Readable, if sometimes a little flat. I remember when we were in Rochester I used to read his stories and wish that he would cut loose and lay his guts out there all over the page, for the world to examine and pick apart. But that's not him. Basically, Michael's piece said that after years of languishing, the company's stock had more than tripled in the past six months. Then he quoted a couple of Twin Cities analysts who predicted the stock would go even higher as the company found new uses for the fabric that formed the core of BabySavr. "It appears the company has found a miracle material," one analyst said.

If we were still living together, I would have complimented Michael on the piece at dinner tonight, I thought. We wouldn't have discussed any of the background, however. The brick wall that separates the details of his work from mine would have prevented that. But, for now, anyway, we're not living together. That made me sad. And angry. I felt my blood boil so hard that I couldn't concentrate on what Pace's boss had said. I had completely forgotten about the short items from the cop house that I was supposed to be writing up for Thom, who had snuck up behind me.

"Whatcha got for me, Skeeter?" asked the stealth editor. "Anything 'handy'?"

Slick and Dick, who had just returned from Wisconsin, began to laugh. I ignored them.

"I'm just working on them now, big fella," I said.

"I read that Miss America is speaking at the Boy Scout Jamboree," Slick said.

"I know where those scouts are going after that: straight to their tents. And they won't be reading the manual," Dick piped in.

Then they started talking about my story—or lack of one. "She's gonna get her tit caught in a wringer," Slick said. "But forget her. The funeral home story is a sure sale for 1A."

The funeral home murders had so much drama that I knew it would buy me the time I needed to chase the hand story. The good thing about attention deficit disorder editors is they're easily distractible.

"More tappin' and less yappin,'" Thom told them.

Chapter 17

Having had all I could take of Slick and Dick, I decided it was time to look more closely at Pace. The address in the police report confirmed what her boss had said; Pace Palmer lived in an apartment building that had been converted to condos two years ago. I headed back to Linden Hills to check it out in hopes a neighbor knew something about where she was.

I pulled my car into one of the few open spots on the street, scrambled out and took one giant step across the eighteen-inch pile of snow still left at the curb after the morning plows had gone through. The building was perfectly sandwiched between Lake Harriet a couple of blocks to the east, and Sebastian Joe's, the best independent ice cream store in the Upper Midwest, just one long block to the west. In the winter, Sebastian Joe's sells ice cream cones for a penny for each degree Fahrenheit on the thermometer. One scoop of chocolate chip cookie dough ice cream in a sugar cone would cost about 27 cents today, I figured.

With a heave, I pulled open the front door and found myself in a vestibule separated by another glass door from the building's well-appointed lobby. To the right was an electronic listing of all the building's residents. I scrolled down the list and punched in the number for Palmer, Pace. It rang four times, then kicked in to her answering machine. "This is Pace. Leave a message," her wispy voice suggested.

I stood there for a few minutes, wondering how I was going to get in the building, when I noticed a sign inside the lobby that said "Welcome. Please visit our selection center in unit 115." I tried to push a button for a superintendent to see if I could be let in, but there wasn't a number like that available. A minute later a couple of young men with keys and tape measures on their belts came through the vestibule.

"Doing a lot of work in this building?" I asked.

"There are sixty-five units in here and we've got eighteen more to go," one of them said. "Lots of remodeling going on."

"How many units are for sale?" I asked.

"About half," he replied.

"I was hoping I could get into the selection center," I said. "Can you let me in?"

"S'pose we could," the other young man said. "Go right."

The smell of freshly sawed wood perfumed the hall as I dutifully turned right and headed for 115. The police report said Pace was in 315 so I guessed her unit was similar, but two floors up. If so, her place was tiny, about 500 square feet.

The selection center was a studio with a "bed nook" just off the living room/dining area and a kitchen where you could flip pancakes on the stove with one hand while reaching for the orange juice in the fridge with the other. I wondered if Pace's home had the same green granite kitchen counter tops and paprika-colored cabinetry.

After poking my head down the hall to make sure no one was coming, I took the elevator to the third floor, where I knocked on the door of 315. No answer. No surprise.

A moment later a white twenty-something woman wearing jeans and a tight T-shirt came out of the unit next door, jingling keys in her hand.

"Do you know Pace?" I asked her.

"Yes. Who are you?"

I offered her my card. "My beat is missing persons and Pace is missing."

"I'm Kate. I'm on my way down to the mailbox," she said. "Want to walk with me?"

As we stepped into the elevator she pressed the button for the first floor. "I know her a bit. We used to leave for work at about the same time. Our parking spaces are together in the garage so we ran into each other on a fairly regular basis," she said.

"When was the last time you saw Pace?"

"It seems to me it was late summer. August, maybe, because we talked about winter coming and the joys of scraping frosted windows from cars parked on the garage roof. She said she was going on a trip, to somewhere warm."

I explained about her co-workers reporting Pace missing and the hand in the lake.

"Gruesome," she said. "Why aren't the police investigating?"

"They didn't believe the old man at first, and then the lake froze. It's too dangerous to send in divers and they can't drag it."

"Why do you think it's Pace's hand?" she asked as she put her key in the mailbox marked 317 and extracted a pile of bills and circulars for savings at Bayers Hardware a couple of blocks away.

"I don't know that it is. But she's missing and lived -- or lives -- nearby. I've got a couple of other missing people I'm checking on, too."

"I hope she just decided to extend her trip. Maybe she ran off with the Hunk." She dropped the junk mail in a wastebasket.

"What 'hunk?' "

"A few days before she left I ran into her with this gorgeous man. Curly hair. Kinda short. Spectacular brown eyes. Nice ass. Always wore a light brown leather bomber jacket. In my mind I called him 'the Hunk.' "

"Do you know his name?"

"No. We just passed in the hall. I think I heard her call to him once. Brock? Pock? Sock? Something like that."

"Have you seen him since you saw her last?"

"Nope."

"What about her car? Have you seen it parked next to yours?"

"It's been there the whole time she's been gone."

"Wouldn't she have taken it to the airport?"

"Not necessarily." She opened her phone bill with a grimace. "I have to head back up to my apartment now. You can walk there with me."

"Why not?"

As we rode in the elevator, Kate explained that Pace often talked about the joys of the light rail system when they met at their cars. "I figured she took the bus downtown, then picked up the light rail to the airport. It would cost her $2.75, compared to $25 in cab fare or heaven knows how much in parking fees at the airport."

"What kind of car does she have?"

"Blue. One of those little station wagon types. We used to argue about her bumper stickers."

"What did they say?"

"One was an old 'Wellstone.' "

"You argued about that?"

"No. We argued about the other two. One said, 'Former proud American.' The other, 'I love my country but I think we should start seeing others.' I told her she was a radical. That was the last conversation we had."

We had arrived at the door to Kate's condo and as she put the key in she turned to me. "Sorry I can't help you more. Pace and I weren't exactly close friends, but we were neighbors and I miss her."

I knocked on a few more doors, but no one answered, which didn't surprise me. It was the middle of the day and the units were small but pricey. I didn't hear or see any children. Single professionals were mostly at work during the day, I figured.

As I made my way back to the elevator, I wondered about "the Hunk." And something else I couldn't quite put my finger on. A little discouraged, I hit the down button and stepped into the lobby. I was passing the rows of mailboxes when it dawned on me. I peeked through the window on Pace's mailbox and could see all the way to the back of the mailroom. If she had been gone for months, why wasn't her mailbox overflowing with junk mail?

Chapter 18

I made a quick U turn and tried to turn the knob on the door to the mailroom. No luck. Then I tried to call the manager of the building but only got an answering machine. I left my name and cell phone number, hoping the manager would get back to me soon.

I decided I should take a gander at Pace's car, but the door to the parking ramp wouldn't open for me because I didn't have a magnetized strip card. I was standing in front of her building, freezing and frustrated, when my cell phone rang. It was Katya ."I think you should stay away from the story. Good—

"I've got a video tape I think has Yuri on it," I said very fast before she could get the rest of the "Goodbye" out. That seemed to stop her.

"Where did you get that?" Her interest was suddenly piqued.

"Doesn't matter," I replied.

"When was it filmed?"

"Don't know. It shows a tiger eating a sheep with men watching. I think they're betting. I wonder if one of them is Yuri."

"Is it a white tiger?"

"Yes, it is," I replied. "If I showed you the tape could you tell me if one of them is Yuri?"

"Bring the tape to the store," she said, then hung up.

As I drove to Katya's store, with the videotape nestled in my purse, I thought about what Slick had said. Was he right? Was I getting myself in deeper than I could handle?

Once again I snagged the last parking spot in front of Furs of Siberia and dumped an hour's worth of quarters in the meter. The metal security door squeaked when I walked in.

Katya, who was showing a large lady a large fur, motioned for me to wait. Half an hour later, the lady left the store without buying anything. "Come with me," Katya said, then led me to the back of the store.

"Give me the tape," Katya said.

She stuffed it into a VCR player, then fast-forwarded through the static until the tiger roared. Her face was impassive as she watched the tiger shred the sheep.

"Is Yuri on the tape?" I asked.

"Yes."

"Which one?"

"That's him in the back," she said, disgustedly.

I stopped the tape and looked closely at the man she indicated. He was about six inches shorter than the others and balding. His body language made me think he was identifying with the sheep.

"Who are these guys?" I wanted to know.

"Some of his friends," she replied.

"What are they doing?"

"Reinforcing their manhood." With a slight smile, she waved her long, cherry-red fingernails at the video screen. "Where did you get this?"

"In Moose Meadow," I replied.

She removed the tape from the machine and put it in a drawer, which was just fine with me. It meant I didn't have to account for ill-gotten goods.

"Leave," she said, and walked me back to the showroom.

She was ushering me to the door when the large lady she had been helping earlier returned to the store. "I think I'll take the mink, after all," the lady said to Katya.

"Of course," Katya said, pasting a huge smile on her face and turning her attention to the customer and away from me.

As I stopped to watch the tableau I noticed a small, curly-haired woman in a smock watching me watch the scene. She gave me a smile and then, very subtly, motioned for me to follow her.

We walked through a long corridor with wooden floors that

had been there since the 1890s.

"What's your name?" I asked.

"BeeBee McGee," she said with a voice even deeper than Katya's.

The corridor was musty and dusty. I glanced in open doors as we walked. Skins of formerly living animals covered tables. We took turns down two more corridors and arrived at a heavy metal door. When she applied her thumbprint to a pad on the door I heard the click, click of a moving deadbolt.

Inside was what I imagined a CIA office would look like. One whole wall was dedicated to security cameras with a half-dozen views of the area, including a great shot of my car parked in front. Nothing unusual there, I thought, but then I looked at the other end of the room. An electronic world map covered the wall, with dots blinking in about six places, including Minnesota and Siberia. On a desk in front of the map were all kinds of blinking boxes and a laptop.

"I wouldn't have thought the furrier business was so high-tech," I said, motioning to the hardware.

"It is," she said with a faint Eastern European accent.

'Why are you showing me this?" I asked.

"Because bad things are happening here. Things that Yuri would never have allowed. It's Katya's doing."

Just as quickly she pushed me from the room and out a side door.

"Find Yuri," she whispered.

My mind swirled like an eddy of snow as I headed back to the office. Why all the fancy stuff in Katya's office? It looked like a lot more than a top-of-the-line security system. Why the map with all the electronic pinpoints? Is she tracking furs on the hoof?

Why didn't Katya seem surprised, or repulsed, by the scene of the tiger devouring the sheep? Had working with furs made her blasé about the sordid side of nature? Watching her, I got the sense that she knew who the men were, including Mr. Pinstripe, who looked like the kind of guy who would have use for the fancy gadgets in her office. What's the scam?

I needed to learn more about tigers.

Chapter 19

Slick and Dick have told me, to the point of nausea, that the digital age has made reporting easier and reporters lazier. Key in a couple of words and *voila,* a lot of what you need to know is right there. Don't even need to get out of your little blue wheeled chair to visit the newspaper's research center, or "morgue," as Slick likes to remind me.

On the other hand, I have argued more than once, the digital age has made reporters more accurate. Spell somebody's name wrong, throw it online along with your email address and you can count on receiving half a dozen indignant missives from readers more than happy to provide the correct spelling, along with a lecture on how the media are just plain stupid. When that happens I make the correction in the file, and hope the name is spelled right the next time. Sometimes it is, sometimes it isn't.

Anyway, I started searching the paper's database. I typed in "white tiger." Turns out, a tiger expert works at the Minnesota Zoo. Who knew? I placed a call and set an appointment then headed for the parking ramp. I drove south on Cedar Avenue, across the Minnesota River, then followed the brown Zoo signs. I was about twenty minutes early so I parked in the lot with some other cars while I jotted down the questions I planned to ask him. A few minutes later another car pulled up next to mine and a man got out.

"Where can I find Geri Fitzgarrald?" I asked.

"You're parked next to her truck. She's probably in the building."

I looked to my right. There sat a red Toyota 4Runner that had to be fifteen years old. Rust covered it like end-stage melanoma.

Judging from her mode of transportation, I expected a woman who had dedicated her professional life to tigers to be a big gal with a full head of hair and a booming voice. I left my car and trudged to her building. A young woman directed me to her office. I knocked softly on her open door so I wouldn't startle her as she stared intently at her computer screen.

"Take a seat," she said, without taking her hands off her keyboard. "I'll be right with you."

I had imagined wrong. Geri Fitzgarrald was shorter than I, prematurely gray, skinny and soft-spoken. She did, however, wear a tiger-print blouse with jeans. Her office looked like a tiger's roar had shaken everything loose a long time ago and she hadn't gotten it put back together. Manila file folders poked from half the drawers in the 1960s-era black filing cabinets. Copies of Cat News were scattered over several piles of indeterminate matter atop what could have been a desk. I wasn't sure. Huge, spectacular pictures of tigers covered the wall.

"Let's go for a walk," she said after finally pulling her head from her computer screen.

We headed for the zoo's Northern Trail, the snow crunching under our boots. I took in the sight of a moose, half a dozen caribou and wolves before we got to the tiger exhibit.

"Let's turn in here," she said. "This is my favorite spot in the zoo."

We walked along a bridge built out above the tiger lair. Looking down at trees caked with snow gave the lair an ethereal feel, something I had never associated with a tiger before. I jumped when a flash went off a few feet in front of us. Do paparazzi chase tigers?

"That was a camera trap," she said. "Don't let it scare you."

"What's a camera trap?"

She explained that we had broken an infrared beam across the walkway. That had triggered an automatic flash and a photo of us.

"You photograph your human visitors?" I asked.

"We have that set up to show visitors how the system works," she said. "We use it in the wild to study tigers."

She pointed to a television screen in the exhibit at the end of the walkway. I looked at my picture, then turned away. I don't like being reminded how silly I look with my red nose and my furry-but-warm hat.

"What brings you to the zoo?" she wanted to know.

I explained I had seen a white tiger in a cage and wondered where it could have come from, what it was doing there and what was involved in keeping a tiger.

"If it was really a white tiger, it was unusual," she said. "They don't exist in the wild."

Fitzgarrald explained that because white is poor camouflage for tigers in a jungle, most have died out. "White tigers are only created in captivity and then it's through a lot of inbreeding. About 80 percent of cubs conceived that way die. And the ones who live are pathetic."

"What do you mean 'pathetic'?" I asked.

"Scoliosis, immune deficiencies, cleft palates, crossed eyes," she said with a sad sigh. "Tell me about the one you saw."

I told her the tiger I saw looked healthy, but skinny. "I could see his spine clearly and it was straight. Why would someone in Moose Meadow, Minnesota, want to keep a tiger? Why would someone anywhere want to keep a tiger, except in a zoo?"

Pelts. That's what most tiger traffickers are after, Fitzgarrald said. Private owners of tigers often breed them, then kill them for their skins. With a sad shake of her head, Fitzgarrald recalled going along on a bust of a private owner on a farm near Moose Meadow. She said the guy had twelve tigers in outdoor cyclone-fenced enclosures over dirt. The stench from a barrel filled with the road kill tiger food was overpowering. He never cleaned their cages, so the rain, urine and feces, along with a leftover bone, were rotted in them.

"You know how cats are fastidious? Well, these tigers had stopped cleaning themselves."

"Tell me about the owner," I said.

"Major league punk. A million tattoos, studded belt with black jeans and boots. Long, greasy hair. Package of Lucky Strikes rolled up in the sleeve of his T-shirt." Fitzgarrald shook her head laughing at the cigarette-package stereotype.

"In those conditions I'd expect the tigers to stop reproducing," I said.

"Tigers are a product of their hormones," she said. "Ever see a cat in heat? She'd have sex with a sofa."

"Is that how a guy like that would end up with a dozen tigers?" I asked.

Fitzgarrald heaved another sigh. "The problem is that people breed tigers trying to get the one tiger that will make them money, and then they get stuck with a litter of worthless cubs. Cubs are cute. Photographers sometimes use them as props."

I flashed back to the button worn by my waitress at Aunt Bea's.

"Then the cubs grow up, and the traffickers have a tiger by the tail, literally," she said. "When they become sexually mature they have a growth spurt. A male can get up to 400 pounds. If they're fed properly—at least fifteen pounds of meat every day—they can live twenty years."

I thought about the guys I had seen in the videotape. They didn't quite fit the picture of the punk Fitzgarrald was painting, especially Mr. Pinstripe.

"The tiger I saw seemed underfed but it wasn't treated as badly as you describe," I said. "Is there a different use for tigers?"

"I've heard of people who have paid upwards of $100,000 for a tiger as a pet," she said. "A rare, healthy white one would go for more than that."

"Who would have that kind of money and want a tiger?"

"Mike Tyson had one. Michael Jackson had one."

"If they're not fed, can they turn dangerous?"

"They're dangerous no matter what," she said. "If they're underfed, they'll eat anything they can get their jaws around."

We returned to her office so she could print out some articles for background information for me. While her printer whirled, I took another look at her workplace. Her computer screen flashed a map of Russia with markers scattered about.

"What's this?" I asked.

"A couple of years ago we tagged tigers for the Russian

government, then used a global positioning satellite to track them," she said. "That's a map of where they all were six months ago."

I stared at it a few more minutes. It looked an awful lot like the map I had seen in Katya' office.

Chapter 20

Even though it was a long stretch from a hand fished from Lake Harriet to a tiger operation, I wondered if somehow they were related. Or if Pace Palmer were tied to one, or even both.

When I went back over my notes I found something I had scribbled down that might help me learn more. I had asked Fitzgarrald how illegal tiger traffickers found their customers. Chat lines, she said. Could it be as simple as that?

I pulled up Google and punched in "tigers for sale." I couldn't believe what popped up on the screen: Bengal, one year old, female. Housebroken, gentle. $28,000. Contact information followed a picture of a yellow tiger looking mournfully through a cyclone fence. Housebroken? I laughed out loud. I'll just bet.

I spent three hours scrolling through the offerings. This was my favorite line: "It is wise to acquire information on Bengal tigers prior to buying kittens." No kidding.

I read through chat rooms until I was as cross-eyed as a white tiger. I was just about ready to log off when this item caught my eye: "MN Frog, email me so we can discuss."

MN, huh? Could it be our own Mr. Pinstripe? I wanted to remain anonymous, so I set up a new Hotmail account—tigress007@hotmail.com—and sent a message: "Wanted: White Tiger. Will Pay Big $$$$$$" then waited for a response.

The reply came back far faster than I had expected. Ten minutes later the email said, "I could put you in touch with a white tiger. How much have you got to spend?"

"I could do $100,000.00," I wrote back.

"Call," it said, with a phone number with a 218 prefix, the code for Moose Meadow.

If I called using the newsroom phone the paper's name would show up on the caller ID. Same if I used my cell phone. I needed a pay phone, few of which exist any more.

"You guys know where I can find a pay phone?" I asked Slick and Dick.

"Calling a lover and you don't want us to eavesdrop?" Slick asked, peeking over the top of his *Wall Street Journal.*

"Yeah, that's it," I replied. "Where's the phone you use to call your sex therapist?"

That drew a chuckle from Dick. "There used to be a pay phone on the skyway near the government center. Don't know if it's still there."

I put my shoes back on and headed down in the elevator, through the tunnel to City Hall, up a flight of stairs then down a corridor that runs under a water fountain to the government center then up two escalators to the skyway level. Looking around, I saw a stand for coffee and pastries, a few cops and a lot of people dressed in office casual briskly headed for their next appointment, but no pay phone. Twenty minutes later, I was still wandering around the skyway system looking for a phone. I knew the phone company had removed some pay phones because cells had cut into their use, but this was ridiculous. Finally, I found one, next to the restrooms in the basement of Dayton's. (Actually, they call it Macy's these days, but it was Dayton's when I was a kid, before it was Marshall Field's, and as far as I'm concerned it will always be Dayton's.)

I fished through my purse looking for change, then dropped two quarters into the phone and dialed the number. A man picked up on the first ring.

"Yes," he said.

"This is Tigress. You said to call."

"What are you looking for, Tigress?" he asked with just a hint of an accent. Was it Russian?

"A white tiger, male," I said.

"Why male?"

"Because I'm a tigress," I purred.

"Why white?"

"Because they're unusual," I said.

"What's that to you?"

"Look. I've got money. That's explanation enough. Do you have a white tiger for sale, or not?" I'm not good at prolonged purring.

"I need to see your green," he said.

"I need to see your tiger," I said.

"He's very gentle," he said. "I think you'll like him."

Yeah, I just bet.

"Where is he?"

"Do you know Moose Meadow?" he asked.

"Yes, I know Moose Meadow," I said. Do I know Moose Meadow? Oh boy.

"Meet me in Aunt Bea's restaurant tomorrow. Noon," he said, and then hung up before I could ask any more questions.

Now all I had to do was come up with a plausible story for why I didn't have the money.

Chapter 21

Lunch time. I debated buying a sandwich and eating at my desk, again, but that can be a mistake. Besides getting yet more crumbs stuck in my keyboard, it puts reporters in the unfortunate position of looking like fish to eagle-eyed editors who need a body for some career-snuffing task. Instead, I texted my friend Lucy Quinlivan, who covers the courts, to see if she was free for a quick bite.

"Waiting for jury. So sure," she texted back.

We met at The Little Wagon, a restaurant and bar near the newsroom and the courthouse. The place was legend. Back in the days when reporters worked out their anxiety through liquor therapy, The Little Wagon was the watering hole of choice. Cops and politicians hung out there too. Every editor knew the phone number to the Wagon by heart because it was the best place to find reporters, wayward and otherwise. But it was mostly empty today. The cuts in the newsroom had led to cuts at the Wagon. And more than a few reporters had changed to a new therapy: yoga.

"If you and Michael break up, what's that mean for the rest of us?" Lucy asked. "You guys are the perfect couple. By the way, Happy Valentine's Day. "

"I told you, we're not breaking up." I opened three little white plastic tubs of half-and-half, poured it in my coffee, then gave it a stir with my spoon. "He's still at the house, some days."

"He told you he's leaving you," she said. "Sounds like splits to me. And how did you ever get the presence of mind to flat-out tell him you didn't believe him?"

I had wondered that myself. Maybe it was the article I read

about a year ago in the Modern Love section of the *New York Times.* The author said that when her husband had informed her of his departure plans she told him, "I don't buy it." The essay resonated with me. I clipped it and stuck it in a file. I don't know if it was foreshadowing, kismet or dumb luck, but I remember thinking that was how I hoped to react if, God forbid, the same thing happened to me. That's what I told Lucy.

"Well, I don't buy it from you," Lucy said. "You know there's an attorney who handles about half the divorces in the newsroom. Do you want his name?"

"No," I said. "At least not yet. I'm going to give Michael some time before I get a lawyer."

Preferring to share newsroom gossip, rather than be the center of it, I changed the subject. Talk of a merger between the Minneapolis and St. Paul newspapers had gotten louder lately. Because she covered courts and talked to lawyers and judges all day long, I checked in with her often.

"What's the latest on a possible merger?"

"Same old, same old," she said. "Neither paper has enough bucks to buy the other."

"Any more on one of them just closing?"

"If I had to pick one, I'd guess St. Paul. Michael would be out of a job. I'm telling you, if you're going to divorce him, you should do it now, while he still has an income."

I asked her what she'd seen in our newsroom lately that might indicate the direction the newspaper's owners might be headed. She said that budgets were tightening daily, and told me a story about an editor who wanted her to do a story about a murder in Duluth, about a four-hour drive away.

"I wanted to go up there, so I could actually see the victim's family when I asked questions," she said. "But the boss wanted a poignant phoner. What are you working on?"

After I told her about the hand which may or may not have been in Lake Harriet, she suggested I take a different tack. If someone without a hand had died last fall—of natural causes—I could reasonably expect that there was no body in the lake, she said. If there's no body in the lake, then I could move on to a new story. Then her phone signaled a text message.

"Jury's back. Gotta go," she said. "Can you get the check?"

Crafting a way to call mortuaries and asking them if they've had any recent customers who would have had a tough time hanging wallpaper just before they died is on my list of less-than-appealing assignments. But being the good soldier that I am, I fired up my computer's search engine and asked for a list of funeral homes in the Twin Cities area. It brought up 416 names and locations. Great, I thought. I've got 416 places to start.

I narrowed the search to just Minneapolis, which brought up eleven funeral homes. That at least made the reporting doable, if not necessarily thorough. People from all over the Twin Cities metropolitan area use Lake Harriet. Somebody could lose a hand in Lake Harriet, die and be buried in suburban Bloomington.

Still, I had to start somewhere. Since one place was as good as any other, I chose the one with my favorite name: Cease, owned by the Cease family.

"Hello, this is Skeeter Hughes from the *Citizen*. I have kind of an odd question. Has your home worked with anyone lately who had lost a hand?"

"What do you mean 'worked with'?" came the reply from a man with a sonorous voice.

"I mean did you prepare a body that was missing a hand?" I replied, thinking again how much I hate this part of the job.

"Is this a prank call? Because if it is, I'll have to call the police."

"No, this is not a prank call. Check your caller ID. You'll see I'm from the *Citizen*. I'm working on a story about a hand that turned up in Lake Harriet and I was wondering if it belonged to someone who died recently."

"I'm sorry but I can't help you Ms. Hughes. The work we do is confidential, except for the information we share with your obituary writers. I'm sure you understand."

"Thanks, anyway." I hung up and dialed another funeral home and then another, repeating essentially the same conversation ten times, until I was sure that even if I called all 416 funeral homes I would not have any more success. Maybe what BJ had pulled up was just a weird fish after all.

On my way home I stopped by the SuperAmerica on Hennepin Avenue and picked up little heart-shaped boxes of chocolates for each of the girls.

Chapter 22

As expected, Michael's official departure had been hard on the girls, but they reacted very differently. Suzy had a million questions while Rebecca was mostly mute on the subject. I struggled with how to answer Suzy reassuringly while drawing out Rebecca to voice her feelings.

"Where's Daddy all the time?" Suzy wanted to know.

"What do you mean 'all the time'?"

"Sometimes he's here for dinner, sometimes he isn't," she said.

As I was about to explain on an eleven-year-old's level, Rebecca walked in. Just as well, I thought, I can talk with them both at the same time.

I had been practicing this moment in my head ever since Michael said he was leaving. The words came out more easily in my imagination.

"Just like kids, adults sometimes go through periods where they're unhappy," I said. "Right now, Dad is unhappy. So he's trying to take a break to figure out why he's sad."

"Is he sad because of us?" Tears were forming in Suzy's eyes.

"No, no, no. Daddy is sad because right now his life isn't going the way he hoped it would. It doesn't have anything to do with you. Daddy still loves you very much. He always will."

"What's wrong with his life?" Suzy asked. "Does he want a puppy?"

"I don't think a puppy will do it." I tried not to laugh.

"Haven't you been listening to him, stupid?" Rebecca finally said. "All he talks about is how bad work is and how he's afraid he's going to get fired and how we don't have enough money for stuff."

"Rebecca's right," I said. "Daddy has a very stressful job in a stressful time."

"You're a reporter," Suzy said. "Are you sad?"

"My job is hard, too, but I react to it differently than Daddy does, because we're different people," I said.

"Can we make Daddy feel better?" Suzy wanted to know.

"You're very sweet to ask, but it's not your job to make Daddy feel better. He's an adult, you're an eleven-year-old. Your job is to be the best eleven-year-old girl you can, and grow up to be a strong, productive woman."

"All this stress-from-work stuff is great, Mom." Rebecca grabbed an apple from the bowl on the table, took a giant bite and chewed while we watched before she continued. "But Dad's not sleeping here any more. I can't remember the last time I saw you guys talking to each other. Has he got another woman?"

There it was, laid out for all three of us to see. Another woman? I prayed to God the only competition I was seriously facing was his badly bruised ego. Another woman? I'd kill him for hitting me with a cliché. I thought back to all the times he had been gone in the past several weeks. Was he really at a Society of Business Editors and Writers conference last month when we kept missing each other's phone calls? And even if he was there, was he with someone else? There was no way I could be sure. But what to tell the girls? The truth.

"I don't think he's with another woman." I looked Suzy, then Rebecca, directly in the eyes. "But if he is, that's something for Dad and I to talk about, not you two. Dad and I have worked out many problems together for years, and that's what we'll continue to do."

Dinner and dishes done, I sat in my early twentieth-century claw-foot bathtub, my knees and shoulders poking through bubbles. The house was quiet, Suzy sleeping, and Rebecca attached as though by umbilical cord to her iPod. I'd set my laptop on the bathroom tile floor and logged onto Pandora.com so I could listen to my favorite music, commercial-free. Tears and snot ran down my face into the bathwater.

As the Dixie Chicks sang "Goodbye Earl," about the missing guy who it turned out no one missed at all, it occurred to me that personally and professionally I was caught in a vortex of missing. At work my beat was literally missing persons. I was in search of a person who was missing a hand. Some of my possibilities were people who were missing. Talk about a double void.

The bigger loss, however, was Michael. I had no idea where he was. Just that he wasn't home on Valentine's Day, which in years past had been a special occasion for us. I remembered the first year he brought home the red heart-shaped box of candies. We took turns choosing pieces until only the coconut-filled ones were left. I laughed because he had chocolate all over his fingers and face. When I licked off his chocolate he pretended to get angry. He said I got more than he did that way. How long had it been since we laughed, really laughed like that? Too long.

Where was he tonight? Was he with someone else? With someone who knew that he refuses to wear pants that aren't roomy in the crotch, that he'd had the half-inch scar on his chin since he fell Rollerblading at eight years old, that he would show up for an appointment half an hour early rather than be late?

Or was he working alone in the newsroom? Triple-checking spellings, figures, addresses because the copy editors had been fired and he knew if he didn't get it right there was no one to correct errors. Was he worrying that he wouldn't have a job in the morning? Was he checking Facebook to see if the girls had posted anything new in the past hour?

Or was he caught up in some nightmare with drugs, or gambling or something more unspeakable than I could imagine?

I didn't know the answer to any of these questions because he was—well…missing.

I thought about how Michael and I met when he was a sports reporter and I was covering education. The high school coach was skimming money off the football budget and paying a local woman to write papers for his star players. Our editor told us to work together on the story.

While I dug through the coach's trash looking for incriminating evidence, Michael scoured the Internet putting together the guy's track record at schools where he had worked earlier. We called each other at midnight, then met to argue for hours about how to frame the story. The coach was a scumbag, an authority figure teaching kids to cheat, I said. No, the coach just wanted to win, Michael said. The resolution between us was the best sex either of us had ever enjoyed.

Michael is the very conservative son of a very conservative doctor at the Mayo Clinic and a top marketing executive at IBM in Rochester. His parents wanted him to be a doctor and marry a doctor, preferably a Republican doctor. That didn't happen.

At twenty-three years old, he married me, then got an MBA and became a business reporter. His parents were put out that I didn't take his name when he finally made me an honest woman. I thought about it, for maybe two minutes, then decided, nah, I've been Skeeter Hughes my entire life. I couldn't see myself answering to anything else. Besides, I figured they would rather I got into trouble using my own name than his. Our girls have both our names, HughesMarks.

My hot bath had cooled to lukewarm as more questions bubbled through my mind. Did I want to stay married to him? Yes, for the time being anyway. Forever? Who knows what's forever. Why? Why was I willing to put up with the agony he was causing the girls and me? Because I know that despite his occasional slips into immaturity he is a good man under tremendous pressure.

Am I weak because I refused to fight with him? Well, I've pushed a bad guy to his death before he could push me. I've looked the governor in the eye and asked him when he would resign. I've delivered babies without anesthetic. Nope, I'm not weak.

Am I so desperate to keep our family together I'll put up with his nonsense no matter the cost? No, not desperate. Willing to work, absolutely. But not forever.

The bath had turned cold, the bubbles were gone and my skin was shriveled. Water swirled down the drain, taking my moribund mid-winter Minnesota blues with it. In my head I gave Michael a six-month deadline to get his act together. And the Dixie Chicks were singing "Some Days Ya Gotta Dance."

Chapter 23

FEBRUARY 15

"Yo, Skeeter." Thom sat in his blue chair, leaning back so far he was almost horizontal, his long legs hooked under the desk drawer. He had just left the morning meeting where editors gather to pick apart the newspaper of the day and toss around ideas for future stories. He crooked his finger in my direction. "Time's up."

"What's that mean?" But I knew what he meant.

"It means I can't hold back the tide of editor angst any longer. We need the hand-in-the-lake story. Now. For tomorrow's paper."

I told him it wasn't ready, which of course he already knew.

"That would have been a good excuse in the olden days when we had enough reporters in the newsroom. But with the last round of layoffs, as you know, we're down a dozen bodies. That's120 fingers that would otherwise be writing. We've got to give our readers something to keep them coming back. So make the story ready. Now. Time's up." He picked up his ringing phone with one hand while waving me away with the other.

I returned to my desk by way of Caribou Coffee, where I picked up the Depth Charge—a double espresso shot added to regular coffee—I needed to get my brain working. It was still early and then I typed.

```
By SKEETER HUGHES
A fisherman today is trying to convince
authorities that he pulled a human hand from Lake
Harriet in Minneapolis last October.
```

```
BJ Jones, 70, said he became disoriented by the
sight of the hand and the roar of an airplane
that flew over the lake just as he was reeling
in what he thought at first was a fish. In the
confusion he dropped his rod, reel and catch back
into the lake.
     "I tried to tell the cops, but I don't think
they believed me," Jones said.
     Minneapolis Police Sgt. Victoria Olson said
Lake Harriet had frozen before Jones told officers
about the hand, making a search impossible until
spring.
     Anyone with information about the possible
hand in the lake is asked to call police.
     A cursory inquiry of surrounding funeral
homes did not turn up any recently deceased
individuals without a hand.
     There have been no reported drownings in
Lake Harriet since at least 1986. Use of city
lakes in general has been declining since the
1970s when the Board of Park and Recreation
removed floating docks, according to former
lifeguards.
```

I filed the story to Thom along with a note giving him BJ's phone number so a photog could get a shot of him to go with the story. Then I trotted over to the photo department and talked to my favorite shooter.

"If you get the assignment on the guy who pulled the hand from the lake, try to show his bad eye," I said.

"Why?"

"Because I hate running this story now and I want readers to see that this guy isn't necessarily the most credible fisherman I've ever met."

I stuffed the horrible feeling I had about putting this in the paper as I prepped for my meeting at noon with the guy who thought I was going to buy a tiger from him. An hour later, my cell phone rang as I wheeled my car off Highway 55 and down the gentle slope that leads into Moose Meadow Lake.

"Got two quick questions here on the hand story," Thom said.

"Yeah."

" 'A cursory inquiry of funeral homes'—what's that mean? How many did you call?"

"Half a dozen," I replied, astounded that he would latch onto that aspect of the story rather than how totally implausible it sounded.

"I'll change that to 'calls to six.'"

"Fine."

"You couldn't get anything more out of the cops?"

" 'Fraid not," I said.

"OK, we're shooting the old guy this afternoon. Story'll be online tonight. Right now it's slated for inside the Metro section."

At least the play will be low key, I thought. Maybe no one will notice.

Silly me.

Soon I was parked in front of Aunt Bea's. Before I got out of my car I looked around, half expecting to see the Maserati parked nearby. I saw only a beat-up Nissan truck, a minivan and a Ford Explorer.

I was early and it was too cold to wait around outside, so I headed in and ordered from my favorite waitress.

"Back again for our famous coffee?" she asked.

"Can't live without it," I replied with a smile. "Three creams, please."

"Remember those guys who were sitting in the corner the day you were in?" she whispered as she set a small white porcelain bowl full of one-ounce plastic containers of cream. "I heard them talking the other day. Not that I eavesdrop on customers, but sometimes you just can't help but hear what people are saying while you clean their plates away, you know what I mean?"

"I know just what you mean," I replied. "What were they talking about?"

"Well, you know I thought it was odd because you don't hear people talk about China much here at Aunt Bea's, unless they mean dinner plates. But that's what they were talking about, and I think it was the country they were referring to."

"What were they saying about China, the country?" I asked.

"I couldn't hear it all, of course, but it sounded like they were going to get a shipment of some kind from there," she whispered again.

"Shipment of what?"

"I couldn't tell exactly," she replied. "Do you think it was drugs or guns or something like that?"

"Beats me," I said.

With that she just shook her head and walked away muttering to herself something about "some people's children."

Mr. Pinstripe strolled to the corner table where I had seen the two brothers. He ordered a cup of coffee and opened the Wall Street Journal on the table. It's so good to see someone reading a newspaper these days, even if it is a bad guy, I thought.

"I think you've got something white that interests me," I said, pulling up a chair opposite Mr. Pinstripe and sitting down.

A man and woman seated nearby turned their heads to watch me sashay to his table. Then she said something to him and he nodded. You can't order a cup of coffee in Moose Meadow without becoming part of the local gossip, let alone talk to a tiger trafficker.

It was easier to study him while sitting close than it had been from behind a tree several feet away. His eyes were bear brown, his hair panther black. His features were fine, almost effeminate. He reminded me of a very young Omar Sharif in *Dr. Zhivago*.

"Do you often conduct business by email?" he asked.

"For something like this, I do. Where's the white tiger?"

"You must be patient. How do I know you will take care of something as precious as this?"

"My client has the money," I lied. "He has the space, and he knows how to get the expertise to take care of a white tiger."

"Who is 'he'?"

"I'm not at liberty to say," I replied. "But I can tell you he has a name you would recognize, especially if you follow the Timberwolves."

That got his attention. He folded his paper, dropped five dollars on the table and pushed his chair away. "Follow me," he said, and then headed for the door.

I could feel the eyes of the couple track my departure. When we got outside Mr. Pinstripe pulled out a cigarette and lit up. It was all I could do to stop myself from bumming one from him.

"Be here with the money this time tomorrow and we can do business." He walked away leaving a trail of smoke behind him.

I stood there a minute, inhaling the scent, remembering how much I used to enjoy it. After the memory passed, I looked up and down the street to see if he got into a vehicle, but he was gone. The couple from Aunt Bea's was sitting in a warming sedan.

My cell phone chirped again as I drove back to the newsroom. A glance at the caller ID told me it was a photographer. I thought about ignoring it. Distracted driving is dangerous, we've told readers repeatedly. But, then again, it might be something important.

"Skeeter here."

"Bad news," said the voice of my favorite photog. "The powers that be aren't happy with a simple shot of BJ's bad eye. They want video to put online with the story. Tonight. We're talking with him at six. Should be up by about nine. Thought you might want to know."

"Thanks for the tip." I hung up before some cop saw me on the phone. Great, I thought. The story I had hoped would get buried with a small picture of BJ with his cloudy eye had been elevated to online video status, where it would get much more play than it deserved. My credibility with readers would be tied to his. I like BJ, but I'm still not positive the hand-in-the-lake story isn't just some creative way to put a little excitement in his life.

I hit the driver's wheel with the heel of my hand as I pulled into the paper's parking ramp. "Shit."

Chapter 24

"Ms. Hughes, this is Officer Joseph Black," said the voice on my phone. I'm with the U.S. Fish and Wildlife Service."

Now what could this be about, I wondered. OK, all right, he had me. I went fishing last August without a license. Maybe I pulled in more than my limit. How does he know?

"How can I help you, Officer Black?"

"My partner and I observed you in Moose Meadow meeting a person of interest to us," he said.

I flashed back to the couple at Aunt Bea's. I thought they were just nosy locals.

"What do you mean 'a person of interest'?"

"I think it would be better if we discussed this in person," he said.

This could be fun, I thought. Seldom—never, in fact—do I get a call from the feds. On rare days a local cop, such as my buddy Sergeant Victoria Olson, will give me a jingle to ask a question I don't want to answer. But an enforcement official from the government of the United States of America? Sure never happened when I was covering Land o' Lakes. I must be coming up in the world. Maybe Interpol will reach out on my cell phone.

"There's a coffee shop near the Hennepin County Government Center, just before you get to the skyway," I said. "Meet me there."

At the agreed upon time I bought myself a large latte—which I planned to list on my expense sheet, since it would be part of meeting a potential source—and took a seat at one of the tables I had passed while looking for a pay phone. Cops, lawyers and government types were everywhere, which made me more comfortable. Maybe some local would see me with the feds. That would definitely up my rep. As I stirred my latte a man and a woman, dressed in business casual, took the chairs opposite me.

"Been in Moose Meadow lately?" I asked them.

The man, whom I assumed to be Officer Joseph Black, was tall and skinny with the longest arms I've ever seen. I imagined him casting a fishhook a mile into a lake. The woman with him was five feet tall, at best, with short blond hair and tiny features. No one would peg her for a Fish and Wildlife officer.

"This is my partner, Officer Claudia Kittock," he said as we three did the obligatory business card swap. "I'm Officer Black."

"You guys want some coffee?" I asked. "The paper's buying."

"No thanks," he said, folding his hands on the Formica tabletop. "You've been a busy reporter."

"Wish my editor thought that," I said.

"What was your business with Anton Smirnoff?" he asked.

"Who is Anton Smirnoff?"

"The man you met at Aunt Bea's."

Well, that cleared up one little mystery for me. I had a name now.

"Like I said, who is Anton Smirnoff?"

"I'm asking the questions here," he said.

I recalled the same response from Sergeant Olson. Geez. A cop is a cop is a cop, I thought.

"So am I," I responded.

This is where these things get tricky. We're both looking for information, but with different, although not necessarily mutually exclusive, agendas. He wants to bust a guy. I want to get in on the bust. My goal was to find the middle ground, and get him to agree to it.

"What is your interest in Mr. Smirnoff?" I asked.

"We think he may be involved in illegal activity. Involving animals."

"Amazing," I replied. "So do I."

"There might be a way we can work together," Officer Black said.

"Could be," I said. "But this is happening a little quickly. You barely know me. Suddenly you want to work with me?"

Black nodded to his partner, who pulled out her iPad, opened a file and passed the device to me. I scanned through what looked like a list of every piece I'd ever written, including plenty I'd forgotten. My bio was so detailed I thought I should ask for a copy to save myself time when I need to brush up my resume.

"You don't have the video of my dogsled ride through Glacier National Park last winter," I said. "You can find it on YouTube."

"We've got it," Black said. "Along with comments from people who say we can trust you."

"Okay, so you do know me," I said. "What have you got in mind?"

"You continue your contact with Mr. Smirnoff, wired with a microphone. When we're ready, you can come along on the bust." As he said it Slick and Dick walked by on the skyway, each of them with a cup of coffee. I gave them a smile and nod.

"I've got a problem with the 'wired' part of that," I said, using my fingers to put air quote marks around the word, "wired."

"What's your problem?"

"That would make me a police informant," I said. "As a journalist I have to maintain my independence to do my work. I work for the newspaper's readers, not the feds. No offense, but anything I find out will ultimately be public information available to anyone."

A silent communication flickered between the two officers. "We won't be taking any more of your time," Black said as he and his partner pulled away from the table.

"Wait," I said. "That doesn't mean there isn't a way we can help each other."

"What have you got in mind?" he said as they both retook their seats.

"My work is done in public," I said. "There's nothing that says you can't follow me around and watch. Obviously you've already been doing that. I'd be willing to keep whatever I learn out of the newspaper until you make your move on Mr. Smirnoff. In exchange, I'd like to go along on the bust."

"That could be arranged," he said.

I told them I had agreed to meet Smirnoff tomorrow. "He wants me to bring the money to Aunt Bea's. I assume he'll take me to the tiger. I'd be happy to pretend I don't see you if you tag along."

Before leaving for work that morning I had put chicken stock and breasts, olives, sliced mushrooms, artichoke hearts, a little tapioca and chopped onion in the slow cooker Michael bought for Christmas. I knew I was home when I opened the kitchen door and the cold of the outdoors mixed with the rich smell of the stew. Ten minutes later the couscous was cooked and the girls and I were sitting around the kitchen table talking through highly serious matters of the day: who wore what to school, how soccer practice was going and how incredibly tough the physics midterm would be. Normal stuff I savored. I cleaned up after dinner and made brownies for a bedtime snack.

Just before midnight I pulled out my laptop and logged on to the paper's website. There it was, the video with BJ's interview, adjacent to the story I had written. He looked right into the camera with his good eye and swore up and down that he had pulled a hand from Lake Harriet. He was actually a little more convincing this time. Maybe the tale was true. Or, maybe he was just getting more practiced at telling it.

I clicked on the comments section on the story. By then it was after midnight and I was shocked to see so many opinions on the story. The story seemed to have hit a chord. Three or four readers said there had been stories floating around for years about a hand in the lake. "Lazy reporting," wrote one. "If you had checked your own library you'd know that some kids told that story forty years ago. It was a hoax then, and it's a hoax now. "Thanks," another reader wrote. "I'll never swim in that lake again." All in all, about 100 people were appalled that the newspaper would report such a claim had been made, a classic case of shoot-the-messenger. But I had to agree. I was the messenger and even I didn't like what I was reading.

Chapter 25

February 16

In the late nineteenth century, hundreds of grain elevators shot up along the Mississippi River to store the hard red spring wheat Midwestern farmers could heap on huge barges and send to market. To ensure farmers a living wage, business leaders formed an exchange so the farmers could offer their grains together, instead of competing against each other. The trading all happened on the fourth floor of the Minneapolis Grain Exchange, built in 1902 on the corner of Fourth Street and Fourth Avenue, the first steel structure in Minneapolis. When markets moved elsewhere and the trading pit finally went vacant, the paper snapped up a 100-year lease at very low rent. The bidding pulpit, the quotation board and a few cash grain tables now act as decorative accents to the *Citizen* newsroom. The acoustics are horrible, but you can't beat the space for charm. The ceiling is three stories high and the place is solid oak. Huge fans circle lazily overhead, stirring up dust over the workers below.

Unfortunately, it didn't take the newsies long to turn the place into a mess. Paper, paper, everywhere. Old news releases, commission reports going back a decade, copies of newspapers from other cities. All of this stacked on top of file cabinets that are already stuffed with the same, only ten years older. The piles of paper in the *Citizen*'s newsroom are bad enough to have caused the fire marshal, heart palpitating, to issue warning after warning followed by threat after threat to close the place down if it's not cleaned up. Meanwhile, we inhale the paper dust that the room's clogged air filters gave up on years ago. We may or may not have ink in our veins, but we definitely have paper particles in our nostrils.

Since the cleaning staff was laid off, and journalists were told to empty their own wastebaskets, the mice have moved in. As an experienced professional trained to observe, I can tell you that people really do shout "EEEEEK" when a mouse scampers by. This is where I spend more than half my waking hours.

My eyes felt like they had sand in them as I dragged myself out of bed and off to work in the morning. But Thom was quite chipper, at least for him.

"The big guns loved the fisherman story," was how he greeted me first thing.

"Great," was all I could say. Even my third coffee couldn't get my blood moving. I hadn't even noticed that Slick and Dick were missing from their usual stations, at least not until I called up the early budget for tomorrow's paper. Apparently some guy had turned up stuffed in a large trashcan in the western suburbs, and they were hot on the story. Well, I had some leads to chase, too, I thought.

I tried to call Katya but got only an answering machine at Furs of Siberia, listing location and hours and urging me to leave a message, which I did, asking her to call me back. I was just about to make another call when my cell phone rang. It was my new favorite from Fish and Wildlife, Officer Black.

"I'm sorry it didn't work out," he said. "If it helps, you need to know it wasn't your fault."

"What didn't work out? And what wasn't my fault?"

"Oh, I thought you reporters knew everything the minute it happened. We executed a warrant on Mr. Smirnoff this morning just before dawn."

"You what? I thought I was going to be in on the bust. That was our deal."

"I'm really sorry, Ms. Hughes. My partner and I argued hard that you should be included. I told my boss you were part of the deal. But then officers found Mr. Yudeshenka's body in the trashcan and the case suddenly took on an urgency. We had to move quickly.

Good thing we did, too."

"Wait a minute," I said. "The guy in the can is Yuri Yudeshenka?"

"That was the preliminary identification," he said.

And Slick and Dick were out there at that very moment working my story.

"And why, may I ask, was it 'a good thing' that you moved so quickly, without my involvement?"

"We netted quite a haul."

"What did you get?"

"There will be a release out within the hour," he said.

That kind of smugness I might have expected from the FBI, but Fish and Wildlife? Give me a break. I had to find a way to salvage at least something from this fiasco.

"Officer Black, you owe me," I said through gritted teeth. "You know my work. If you expect any kind of relationship with me in the future, you had better tell me, now, what you got from the arrest of Smirnoff.

"A tiger. White. From Russia, it appears. That makes this an international case. Interpol is interested. There was also several thousand dollars in cash. Furs from other endangered species, and a half a dozen stolen cars."

Good thing I hadn't spent a lot of time figuring out how I was going to convince Smirnoff I actually had money to pay for his tiger.

"Thanks," I said, and hung up the phone with a slam.

"Thom," I yelled as he happened to be passing within shouting distance of my desk. "The guy in the trash can is related to a bust the feds made this morning in Moose Lake. I got some detail."

"Fine. File ASAP," he said.

I was just finishing the final touches on the story as Slick and Dick appeared. Absentmindedly scratching his crotch as he slid into his chair, Slick was telling Dick that it was a good thing "that Russkie was such a little guy, otherwise he wouldn't have fit in the trash can." Dick thought that was hilarious.

Thom was beside their desks in seconds. "So who killed him?

How did the killer do it? What did he use? A garrote? A knife? A gun? How did it work? What does it sound like when somebody dies that way? Find a medical examiner or somebody who can tell you that. What's his wife say? His kids? Did he have kids? Has anybody even talked to his wife or kids? How old are they? Are they glad the old bastard is gone or are they heartbroken they'll never see him again. Do I have to think of these things all by myself? Who's on this anyway? How about a story on Rottweilers? We keep hearing about pit bulls attacking kids, but what about Rottweilers? They're vicious, too. My neighbor has a Rottweiler and I swear one day he's gonna kill every cat, if not every kid, in the neighborhood. Vicious, I'm telling you, vicious. What do they usually weigh? What do they eat, other than squirrels, I mean? How long do they live? What would it take to kill one of those? Would a crowbar do it? A screwdriver? Find out. Readers want to know. Or raccoons? There must have been ten of 'em in our trashcan last night. Woke us up. Definitely an issue in the city and the suburbs of interest to readers. My kids think they're soooo cute, but not when I have to clean up all the crap they spread all over after they've finished picking through the dumpster. Which reminds me, dumpster. Did Yuri die in a dumpster or a trashcan? Was there some pop psych message in where he died? Was somebody trying to say he's trash? Can we get some expert to talk about that? Why didn't you guys think of that? Get on it? Deadline's coming. Tick. Tock."

Done with Slick and Dick, for now, Thom turned to a different reporter on whom he unleashed his I-haven't-had-my-Ritalin-yet-today tirade.

"How'd you guys get this story so early in the morning?" I asked the Joker and the Penguin. "I'd have thought you would still be tucked in bed on such a cold morning."

"Sources, Skeeter," Slick said. "It's always good to have sources."

"And let me guess? The deceased's name was Yuri Yudeshenka, correct?" I asked.

"Well yes, it was," Dick said.

"Did you actually see the body?" I asked.

"This is a tough business and sometimes you have to see some unpleasantness," Slick said. "Yes, yes we did see the body. "

I took a deep breath before asking the next question.

"How many hands did he have?"

"Two," Slick and Dick said at the same time.

Chapter 26

Two hands. Yuri turned up with two hands. Yikes! I had never even spoken with the guy and I felt bad for him. Not bad that he had both his hands, but that his final resting place was a trash can. I took his picture down from the cloth wall of my half-cubicle and stared at it.

"Hey, Slick, not that it really matters, but did the cops find Yudeshenka upright in the trash can?"

"Actually, he was ass-up," Dick, who often finished Slick's sentences, replied. "Why?'

"I don't know. I'm just trying to get a picture for what might have gone on. Cause of death?"

Slick said the official word was an autopsy was pending. "But when the victim's head is separated from his torso at the neck, it's a good guess that foul play was involved."

What happened to you, Yuri, I wondered. Did you get crosswise with Smirnoff the Panther? How did Katya figure into all this? She made it clear when I first spoke with her that she was done with you.

My cell phone binged that I had a text message: "U O me. Call Sergeant Olson."

Who can turn down something as cryptic as that I thought as I dialed my new best friend.

"So, Victoria," I said when she answered. "I am eager to be in your debt. What's up?"

"Always nice to hear from you," she said. "I was thinking about your buds, Slick and Dick, and how unfair it was that they should have access to information that you might not. So, I thought I'd level the playing field, so to speak. Call it the advancement of the sisterhood."

I'll take a tip anyway I can get it. "So, whatya got for me?"

She said she recalled that I had been asking about Yudeshenka just a few days ago.

"There's a warrant being issued for his wife's arrest, as we speak," Olson said. "She's being charged as an accessory in his murder. Seems she and her boyfriend Smirnoff had an exotic animal smuggling ring and hubby found out about it. Bad for hubby's health."

"How long had he been dead?" I asked.

"Preliminary guess is six to twelve hours," she said.

"But Katya reported him missing months ago," I said. "Where's he been all this time?"

"Good question," she said with half a smile. "We're working on that."

"How did you guys know who to arrest?"

"Seems some Fish and Wildlife guys were tailing Smirnoff. Caught him in the act," Olson said.

I thanked her profusely then hung up to feed the info to Slick and Dick, which got me the number three spot in the byline. It wasn't what I needed to hold on to this great job of mine, but some days a girl's got to work with what's available.

However, the resolution did tell me whose hand wasn't fished from Lake Harriet. Maybe it belonged to Pace, or Amber.

Chapter 27

I checked my voice messages. Angry diatribes from the Linden Hills Business Owners Association, the mayor's office and chamber of commerce giving me hell for the story about the hand in the lake pretty much filled my message box. The comment count online for the story was up to 87.

"I gotta agree with the skeptics," I said to Thom as he passed by. "That piece was awfully light."

"You reported what you know, nothing more," he said. "The story's getting a lot of hits. A few more and it will make it into the top ten most emailed pieces for today."

I took little comfort in that, or in the fact that Slick and Dick beat me to Yuri's body.

"Look, Skeeter, you got a story in the paper," he said. "That's what we do and, with luck, we'll keep doing it for a while longer. What's up with the other two 'missings'?"

I explained I had turned my attention to Pace, who didn't have any mail and whose car had been parked in the same spot for months. She probably took light rail to the airport. There had been an unnamed man hanging around.

It wasn't much.

"I'm working hard on this, Thom." It sounded lame even to me.

"How do you know Pace didn't have any mail?" Thom wanted to know.

"Her mail box is empty."

I explained that I was in her building, had talked to her neighbor.

"How'd you get in? Was it a legal entry?"

That Thom, always worrying about the finer points.

"Yes, it was legal," I replied. "Some workers let me in."

"Wasn't there a story a year or two ago about workers converting a building to condos robbing the tenants?" Thom asked. "Maybe Pace got crosswise with a burglar."

I recalled the same story. Maybe Thom had a point.

"Look into it," he replied. "I can take a little more heat from the big guys who want us all over this hand thing, but not a lot."

Then he turned to Slick and Dick. "A little more tapping and a little less napping, please."

I tried the building manager again, then left a message asking if there had been any burglaries and asked her to call me. Then I thought more about Pace. It looked like her life revolved around work and only occasionally involved a man. I had no idea where, or who, "the hunk" was, so I decided to look a little more closely at her work.

I checked Lexis-Nexis, the Securities and Exchange Commission and Bloomberg.com. There was a fair amount of reasonably reliable information.

Just as Michael's story had said, BabySavr was doing very well. A year ago a university study had credited it with a drop in sudden infant death syndrome, which sent the company's stock value up 12 percent. I'm not a business reporter, so I don't know all the ins and outs of reading balance sheets like Michael does, but the company looked pretty good to me.

When Rebecca was a baby, we had an early scare when she stopped breathing one afternoon just as I happened to check on her while she napped. I gave her a little nudge and she started breathing again, but I was so terrified I called her pediatrician right away. She told me to keep a close eye on her but didn't offer any more advice.

I watched her like a mother hawk for six months and she never had another episode. Eventually, we figured, she outgrew whatever the problem was, but it sure would have been nice to have something like the BabySavr to give us some peace of mind.

I spent another hour staring at the screen trying to find out something that looked out of whack about the company. Couldn't find a thing.

Websites like the ones I was looking at don't post pictures and I really wanted to eyeball the company's founders. More times than I'd like to count, I have picked up annual reports from companies that Michael had left on the floor next to the bed. I recalled that they often had photos of the founders of the company, so I wandered back to the section of the newsroom where business reporters sit.

Companies whose stock is owned by a few individuals—not traded on the stock market—such as BabySavr, are not required by law to give regular detailed accounting of their affairs. But they often publish glossy booklets that give information about the company. It's a way for them to keep their well-polished image in the public eye in preparation for the day when they do sell shares on the stock exchange.

"Have you guys got an annual report for BabySavr around here anywhere?" I asked the business assistant. She directed me to the file cabinet ten feet away, where the reports from privately held companies reside.

I leafed through them all, then came to the last page of the first report. Under the heading, "Our team" was a picture of eight men gathered around a battered wooden rectangular table. Seated in the middle was a silver-haired man wearing a white lab coat. The guy could have been a double for Marcus Welby. I wondered if they'd hired a model for the photo. His smile was benevolent, his eyes kindly. Sitting immediately to his right was a gorgeous brown-eyed younger man with thick curly brown hair, wearing a leather jacket. If ever there was a hunk, this guy was it. The caption under the photo said the men sitting at the table were the earliest researchers with the BabySavr. I matched up the names and found that "the hunk" likely was Edsel Cobb, M.D.

I tried the name on Dex online and came up with no match for a residential listing, but did get an office building address near Fairview University Hospital. At least it was something.

But what was I to do? Call the guy up and say, "Hi, I'm a newspaper reporter looking for Pace Palmer and I think you're the hunk she was dating before she disappeared. Do you know where she is?"

As I pondered that question I looked up and saw Thom half a newsroom away in the afternoon huddle. Unlike the morning huddle, the afternoon meeting—4:00 to 4:20 every day, exactly—is meant to give editors a chance to hash out what they think will be in the next day's paper. I heard Thom pitching a story by Slick and Dick about a bust the cops had made the night before.

"It's timely. A good read. As far as I know we're ahead of the competition on this one," he said.

"Is it above- or below-the-fold good?" the sports editor wanted to know. He had a think piece about the fight over building a new stadium he had already pitched as something that he wanted stripped across the top of page one. If the cops bust story went above the fold too it would likely put a squeeze on the national story that was already set for the top half of the paper.

"Given the other stories possible today, I'd say definitely 1A, but it could go below the fold," Thom, ever aware of newsroom politics, replied.

"I just got a press release about a ladies shaver that doubles as a vibrator," said the Variety editor.

"Sounds like a contender for our Inside & Out page," replied the international editor, who actually drew a round of laughs.

I was only half listening until I heard someone say "Skeeter."

"She's working hard on a missing persons story," Thom replied.

"I heard she's trying to get a HANDle on it," piped up the religion editor. Everyone laughed.

"She's making progress," Thom said. The guy is a master at vague. "But back to the cops piece … ."

I picked up the phone and called Dr. Cobb.

"Physicians On Call," the receptionist answered.

I didn't have to run through the questions because he wasn't there.

"Do you know when he'll be back?" I asked.

"He doesn't come into this office much," the receptionist said.

"I thought this was his office," I replied.

"He works on call for most of the urgent care offices around the Twin Cities," she said with a sigh. "Can I take a message?"

I left my name and phone number.

"What shall I tell him this is regarding?" she asked.

"Tell him it's regarding Pace Palmer." If I didn't hear from him in a day or two, I I'd call him back.

Seldom do people call me back quickly, so I thumbed through the first annual report while I waited. Most companies spend a lot of money on them, putting their best possible face on the company. They're almost always four-color, heavy slick paper booklets with enough pages to swat a fly dead. Usually written by public relations firms, or sometimes by well-paid freelancers, founders want to give potential investors good reason to buy shares of the company. In this case, the annual report was chock full of glossy pictures of smiling, chubby-cheeked babies of most races who had been breathing regularly ever since receiving the BabySavr.

I couldn't find any mention of Pace in the first report, but when I moved on to the second she had joined the "our team" picture, seated just to the right of the chairman. If there was any chemistry between Pace and Cobb, I couldn't read it from their body language in the picture. She sat straight as a lady coached at a charm school, her hands clasped in front of her and resting on the table. I imagined her feet were crossed at the ankle beneath her. She wore a navy suit with a simple navy shell, a pearl necklace and pearl earrings. If there was a ring on any of her fingers I couldn't see it in the picture.

I started to rip the picture out of the annual report, then remembered that the last time I did the biz assistant shot evil-eye daggers at me for weeks. So I made a photocopy of the picture then made sure she saw me return the annual report to its proper place. I headed back to my desk and pinned the photo into the fabric of my cubicle, next to the more recent photo of Yuri that had accompanied Slick and Dick's report of his two-handed demise. Even though he was no longer a candidate, I hadn't taken his photos down. The story didn't feel done yet.

I stared at Pace's picture a long time. Where are you? I wondered. You don't look like the type to head for Aruba, or wherever, without telling anyone. On the other hand, maybe you decided it was time to leave your boring, predictable days behind and see the world. Maybe you browsed through a bookstore one day, picked up 1,000 Places to See Before You Die and realized you hadn't seen any of them. Maybe you decided on the spot that the time to go was now. Maybe you were tired of living a safe life. If that was your decision, then more power to you, Pace, I thought. You go, girl.

Or, maybe the hand didn't belong to Pace. Maybe it belonged to Amber. I realized I needed a picture of Amber so I could ponder her fate, too.

Chapter 28

Snow was falling in huge, quiet clumps as I drove home. Winter is a lovely time of year. It's quiet. It's crisp. It can give a person time to reflect. Reflecting on my life, on the girls, on what might have happened to Amber and Pace. That's what I was doing when some poor son of a bitch slid through a red light and nicked the bumper of my car with a force that sent me sailing into the path of a sanding truck.

Car accidents have a sound all their own. First, there's the thunk, followed by the screech of metal on metal. And then there's an eerie quiet.

What I remember most was that quiet in between. Then the sound of my airbag deploying. My car is small, but very well made. And I was lucky. I had grazed off the side of the sanding truck and spun around to land in a snow pile that had not yet hardened to rock. It cushioned my stop.

The driver of the sanding truck jumped down from the cab and ran to my car. "Are you okay?" she asked. "I've called 911."

I didn't know if I was okay or not. In fact, I didn't know much of anything. Or even care. In some ways, it was a beautiful moment. I was suspended. No pain, no joy, no feeling at all. Just a moment that will be with me the rest of my life.

The hit-and-run driver continued on, disappearing into the darkness.

The scary part was the resumption of sound. The wail of a siren that I knew was approaching for me. The whoosh as my airbag deflated. I heard horns honking as drivers presumably circumnavigated the accident scene while trying simultaneously to see what had happened.

In the darkness I could see the blue and red blinking lights of an approaching police car that pulled in at an angle to mine. "Are you okay, Ma'am?" the officer at my side window asked.

I told him I thought I was all right, as he opened the door to the car. Slowly I extricated myself, moving each limb carefully. He helped me to the back seat of his patrol vehicle, which was warm but smelled slightly of vomit and urine. I hoped it wasn't mine. I sat there for a while, catching my breath and taking personal inventory. All my parts appeared to work, though my forehead hurt and I wiped blood from my nose. I gazed from the window and saw my car stuck in a snow pile facing the wrong way against traffic.

The officer, who looked young enough to still be in high school, took down the pertinent information.

"Did you see the other driver?"

" 'Fraid not," I said. "Did anyone else?"

"Nope. The sanding truck driver just saw him run the light. Didn't catch a license plate."

"Damn."

I told the officer I didn't want an ambulance. I just wanted to go home. I pulled out my AAA card and called for a tow truck. And I called Michael.

"Jesus, Skeeter," Michael said as he drove me home. "Tough day?"

I allowed as how it had been one of my less fruitful. Then I started to babble, about everything I'd been working on, how frustrated I was, how I didn't know where to turn.

"I read your piece about BabySavr," I told him. "Not bad."

He hummed quietly, something I've learned over time is his unconscious way of making a decision.

"What, Michael? What are you thinking?"

"I've wanted to do a story, a real story, on BabySavr for a while," he said. "Months ago I asked for time to look at the company up close and personal."

"And the paper wouldn't give you the time?"

"No. They couldn't spare the body. They need me to keep re-writing releases about great sales." He didn't even try to hide the resentment in his voice.

"Why do you want to do the story?"

"Because something isn't right with those guys," he said.

Chapter 29

FEBRUARY 17

Saturday. Thank God. It had been a long, frustrating week and the missing, including Michael, were still missing. I woke at the usual six a.m. even though I knew I didn't have to get up, get girls up, get us all out the door in time to start another day of work and school. I poked my arms over my head, took a nice leisurely stretch and went back to sleep.

Michael had picked the girls up the night before so I was all alone, enjoying the sweet peace of solitude. Maybe being a single mom wouldn't be so bad after all, I thought.

What to do with this day, I wondered upon waking. I could write the great American novel, but I just wasn't up to it. I needed to do something a little less grand, something more manageable. I lay in bed and looked around, remembering the day when I was pregnant with Rebecca that Michael and I had slapped Wildflower Honey, a bright yellow paint on these walls. He, the meticulous, applied blue painter's tape around all the oak windows and framing for the closet. I, the speedy, dropped the roller in the pan and applied it to the walls, finishing three in the time it took him to tape the place. Rebecca is well into puberty now and the Wildflower Honey bedroom isn't so sunny any more. Time to repaint, I thought, throwing off the covers and heading for the bathroom.

Half an hour and two cups of seriously creamed coffee later I was on my way to Home Depot to buy paint.

"How big is your bedroom?" the helpful fellow in the orange

apron with the white square covering his sternum asked.

Michael had always bought the paint. It hadn't occurred to me to measure the room.

"Big enough for a queen size bed, two dressers, a rocking chair and a standing mirror," I said.

He figured a gallon would be enough for starters.

"Color?"

"I was thinking something in a blue, kinda of like dusk," I said.

"How about Castle Moat?"

I'm a word person. The words, Castle Moat, sounded about right to me. In fact, they sounded perfect. A fortified castle. That's what the bedroom had become. And I was the overseer of the bridge over the moat.

"Ok, mix it up," I said.

I bought a roller, a pan and a small brush. And drop cloths. Lots of drop cloths.

"Need tape?" asked another person in an orange vest who helped gather those items.

"Nope," I said. "Taping takes too much time. I'll just go around the edges with the small brush, then fill in with the roller."

I tuned the car radio to an oldies rock station and sang along at the top of my voice as I drove home. The stresses of the weeks before slipped further away as I belted out one song after another. No one mocked me. No one changed the channel.

After hauling the supplies into the bedroom I made another pot of coffee and began to empty the room. One of the nice parts about our 1921 duplex is two closets in the main—I refuse to call it master—bedroom. I scooped up my wardrobe in three trips and moved it to the living room. What remained of Michael's clothes I put into a plastic garbage bag and hauled it to the back porch, ready to go in the trash.

We've got beautiful hardwood floors covered with a five-by-seven foot rug at the end of the bed and two three-by-two rugs on either side. I rolled those up and put them in the living room, too. Moving the dressers wasn't as easy, alone. I didn't want to drag them away from the wall and scratch the floor. So I retrieved the smaller rugs and put them under the feet of the dressers and pulled them into the center of the room. Moving the bed was even tougher, but with lots of pushing and pulling, the same trick worked. There were enough dust bunnies under the bed to start a herd and build a warren. After sweeping them up, along with a ballpoint pen, a catcher's mitt and my favorite bra that had been missing in action for a month, I covered the bed with the drop cloths. It was lunchtime.

I made myself a cup of Campbell's high-sodium tomato soup and a peanut butter and jelly sandwich to eat while I read the Minneapolis and St. Paul newspapers. Michael had a competently written piece about Medtronic's plans to launch a new product. I checked our business section to see if we had similar news. Nope. Score one for Michael.

Lunch over, I made for the bedroom where I spread out the newspaper I'd just read. So many uses for newsprint, I thought as I placed the paint can on the paper and jimmied open the lid with a screwdriver. The color looked more steel than blue, but I figured the color would come out better after the paint was dried on the wall. With Rush Limbaugh huffing and puffing on the radio—I like to know what the other team is thinking—I began to outline the windows and walls in the room.

I was half done, the lower half, that is, when all that exertion on my body, which usually sits at a computer, began to take its toll. I set the paintbrush on the side of the can and lay down on the bed for a few moments to rest. The mid-afternoon winter sun streamed through the windows, catching the dust motes in full dance. Swirling, spinning and chasing each other they made me think about my life. Was that what I was always doing? Swirling? Spinning? Chasing but never really catching anything? Had I been so caught up in motion that I never actually saw the sunshine right in front of me?

I thought back to a time when I broke my ankle after I slipped on an icy piece of sidewalk and had to spend a couple days on the couch. Rebecca was about six and we had time to read and play games. "I like it that you broke your ankle, Momma," she said to me. "It means you just sit still."

I must have dozed off because the next thing I knew it was getting dark. I sat up with a start and put my foot down fast on the floor, hitting the tip of the handle of the small paintbrush. It catapulted in the air, spraying droplets along its route before landing smack in the middle of the oak dresser that had been my grandmother's.

"Shit," I said to Limbaugh, and grabbed for the brush. Unfortunately, it had already spread Castle Moat all over the oak.

I wiped it up as best I could, then set back to work, finishing the outline of the room. Castle Moat encroached upon only a couple—ok, three or four—spots on the white ceiling. But I didn't get any on the handsome woodwork surrounding the windows.

It was midnight by the time I got to the roller part. My back, arms and legs all hurt and my hair was streaked in steely blue. But I am speedy at that part and the whole room was done by about two a.m.

I stepped back to check my handiwork. The former sunny bedroom now in steely blue reminded me of the inside of a prison cell in the harsh glow of the ceiling light. Well, maybe it will look better in the morning, I thought.

Then I had another thought. So this is what it's like to be a single woman. I hate it. I went to the back porch and retrieved Michael's clothes.

Michael didn't come in when he dropped the girls off about noon the next day.

"I smell paint," Suzy said. "Stinks."

Rebecca followed her nose to the bedroom. "What did you do, Mother?"

"I painted the bedroom. What do you think?"

"I think you're a bitch," she said.

I was taken aback. Rebecca had never called me that before, at least not to my face.

"I think it's…not too bad," said Suzy, who stood behind Rebecca.

"Yeah, you would," Rebecca said to Suzy. "You're always sticking up for mom. How come you never think about dad? It's still his bedroom, too, ya know, even if he doesn't sleep with her any more."

I thought back to when as a toddler Rebecca threw a temper tantrum. She was angry with me for some reason I no longer remember. I do remember she tried to hit me with her tiny fist, her face scrunched up in a tight little ball, like a balloon that had puckered after losing air. I didn't yell at her, spank her or give her a time out. Instead, I stepped away, out of her reach. Then I went about my business, ignoring her display. I refused to reward her outburst with attention.

Like that tantrum twelve years ago, this one wasn't really about me. It was about Rebecca's anger at Michael's midlife crisis, the threat it posed to our family, to her. In my heart, I felt her pain. I wanted to lash out, too, to cry and yell and swing my fists. But one of us had to be the adult, and I was the senior family member in the room. I began to pick up the drop cloths.

Rebecca stormed off to her room, slamming the door behind her. The low murmur of her voice as she talked on the phone to somebody – was it Michael? – seeped through the walls.

"She's talking to that boy," Suzy said.

"Which boy?"

"The one she talks to every day on the bus on her cell phone. He doesn't go to her school, I think," Rebecca said. "Or at least he doesn't ride the same bus."

I told Suzy that I expected Rebecca to cool down, even though it's hard.

"She called you a bitch, mom," Suzy said.

"I know. She shouldn't have. I'll talk to her about it later when she's not quite as angry."

"You're not a bitch," Suzy said. "But you shouldn't have painted the bedroom. Especially such an ugly color."

I had to laugh. Suzy was right, on all counts. And I told her so.

Chapter 30

February 18

Monday. A whole week later and I wasn't any closer to coming up with a body to go with the hand. I needed to go back to the beginning so I called my buddy BJ, the hand fisher, and made an appointment to talk at our favorite coffee place after I picked up the loaner car from the body shop.

I love Linden Hills, even if I can't afford to live there. I've watched the neighborhood for years. A generation ago it was filled with people who were interesting, not moneyed. They were potters and painters and folks who made gourmet dog food for a living. For a while it was called the land of 10,000 golden retrievers because of a particularly prolific pair whose owner lived in the neighborhood. There were a few very big houses and more small houses and rental duplexes. As the real estate market began to take on almost mythic proportions, the small houses were bought by people who tore them down and built very big houses on their lots, selling them for three or four times what they paid for the small houses. A big part of the attraction to the area was nearby Lake Harriet.

During the warm months, sailboats skim the surface like swans as runners pace out 2.8 miles around. Each summer Sunday morning a different church offers services at the band shell overlooking the lake. People have married on her shores, learned to swim in her waters, fed generations of ducklings. Believing the mental picture of a hand fished from Lake Harriet took some work.

I was palming my latte—time to get a little more calcium in

my diet—when I heard the shuffle of his rubber boots on the wood floor. BJ pulled the wooden chair along the mud-speckled floor and landed with a plop.

"That's some shiner ya got there, Skeeter." The rip in the T-shirt he had worn the last time we spoke was a little bigger and he smelled a little worse. His rheumy eye was rheumier. "What's the other guy look like?"

"Don't know," I said. "He took off after running a red light. How are you?"

"Lotsa people saw that video about me and the hand." Alcohol mixed with the nicotine of his breath. "I'm a celebrity."

"How's that working out for you, BJ?"

"They still don't believe me." He shook his head a bit, swirled his coffee.

"Gotta tell you, BJ, I'm stuck. So far I got no proof that anybody is in that lake."

"Whaddya expect me to do about it? I saw what I saw, I'm telling ya. I pulled a hand out of the lake. Doesn't mean there's a body to go with it. Maybe somebody just found a hand in the trash and threw it in the lake. I don't know."

Great, I thought. He's turning irascible on me. I stirred my coffee with a force so strong it could have bent the spoon, hoping to vent my frustration. Didn't work.

Still, something nagged at me. I just couldn't let go of this story. Was it because I desperately needed a good story to hold onto my job? Yes, but that wasn't the entire reason. There was something else.

BJ sipped his own coffee while watching me critically as I thought. Something hung between us like a curtain of moss.

"Ya know," he finally said, "I wasn't going to bring this up because then you'll really think I'm a crazy old coot. But you know that church at 44th and Upton, just a couple of blocks from here? Called Spirit Community or something like that. There's a guy there who says he can talk with the dead. I even visited him once after my Loretta passed."

He told me he was walking by the church on his way to the lake to fish when he saw the sign for a psychic fair the church put on last Halloween. Loretta had passed a year before and he was feeling lonely, so he stopped in. Half a dozen readers sat at small candle-lit tables beneath the domed ceiling talking in soft tones with the individuals. BJ shuffled up to the only man. "I figured the gals were gypsies, but the guy looked legit."

"What was the guy's name?" I made a mental note to run a check on him.

"Lars." BJ hooted. "Lars Larson. What kind of name is that for a ghost-guy?"

The reader told BJ that Loretta was fine, that she loved him, and reminded him that she had left hotdish in the freezer for him before she died.

"That's when I started payin' attention," BJ said. "How could he have known about the hotdish?"

It's not much of a stretch to imagine a dying wife leaving dinner in the freezer for her husband. Maybe BJ's buddy Lars made it up. Would I do something like that? Nahhhh. I'd be more likely to leave them a lengthy list of names and phone numbers for restaurants that deliver.

"What are you getting at here, BJ?"

"Maybe he can talk to the hand."

I played BJ's idea in my head as I returned to the newsroom. A friend had taken readings with a medium and swore by the results. And, I was at a dead end. First thing to do was check on the Lars Larson fellow, I decided.

My second latte steaming at my side, I ran Larson's name through all the newsroom's databases. Much to my surprise, he turned up in a story written a couple years ago. The cops had turned to him for help in finding three missing University of Minnesota students.

"Although his information was not 100 percent accurate, it did point us in some promising directions," said the detective quoted in the story. Two of the three bodies were found in the Mississippi. Foul play was ruled out. They got drunk and fell in the river. I shook my head in sorrow as I thought about the boys and their families. What were those guys thinking? What agony for their parents. What a waste.

I checked Larson's website. He charged $60 for a half-hour reading. There was no way I could expense that one. This would have to come from my own pocket. And, I had no intention of telling Thom that I was going to consult a medium. He'd laugh me out of the newsroom. No, I'd have to treat Lars Larson as a confidential source, never to be quoted, who would only direct me to the right places to ask the right questions.

Everyone has a website, especially mediums who need to make a buck, and Lars Larson was no different: accepts Visa, MC, Disc and Amex. I made an appointment online and met him in a coffee shop in St. Paul. Didn't want to take the chance that someone from the newsroom might see me.

I arrived a few minutes early, ordered a mocha coffee and took a seat at a table for two in the corner of the crowded shop. I wanted to eyeball him in person before introducing myself. He didn't give me the opportunity. Moments later a guy who looked exactly like the picture on his website walked up to my table. "Skeeter Hughes?"

I allowed as how that was me and invited him to sit down after he got his brew. As he placed his order, I gave him the once over. He was an average-looking white guy of average size wearing nondescript pants and shirt and a North Face black jacket.

"What can I do for you?" I put him in his early thirties.

I told him I was looking for somebody and had hit a dead end.

"I might be able to help you," he said. "A half-hour reading is $60."

Anybody watching us would have thought I was buying some kind of contraband from the way I discreetly pushed three twenties across the table to him.

"You're uncomfortable about this," he said. "You're thinking about leaving."

"Got that right," I said.

"That's normal. I'll give you your money back and we can go our separate ways if you want," he said.

That made a difference for me. What did I have to lose, except $60? "I'll stay."

I told him I actually was looking for three people. He said he needed their names before he could help.

"Yuri, Amber and Pace." I gave him Yuri's name just to see what he'd do with it.

He wrote all three down on a napkin in a vertical column, and then ran his fingers over each name. Eyes closed, he tipped his head down and to the left.

"Could some of these people be dead?" he asked.

"I don't know," I said.

"I'm getting different messages from all three. It's like hearing static on a radio. Some pieces come through and some don't. The females are sending different messages than the male."

So far, I was unimpressed with what he had to say. It's a fair guess somebody was dead here. Saying men gave off a different vibe than women took no special talent. But I kept listening.

"I'm getting a fourth name," he said. "Is there somebody named Harry, or Harriet who connects these three people?"

Had I been on a TV show I'd have spit out my last sip of coffee. But I'm a reporter trained to remain stone-faced during interviews.

"Could be," I said. "What are you hearing from the women?"

"One is fine. But the other is having trouble breathing. Does she have asthma? I feel a constriction in my chest."

"Which woman can't breathe?" I asked.

"Can't tell, but she can't feel anything in one hand. Did one of the women have a stroke? Or a broken arm?"

I restrained a smile. "What about the man?"

"He's quiet. He's here, but not saying anything. Is he a cowboy? He's pulling me west."

Lars' comment was so vague that it didn't really mean anything. Plus, it didn't tell me anything I didn't already know. Moose Meadow is considerably west of St. Paul and the tape I had shown Katya made it clear that Yuri had been there. He couldn't distinguish between Pace and Amber, so that didn't help me either. On the other hand, I had to give him serious points for coming up with the Harry/Harriet connection. There was no way he could know that Lake Harriet was a key component in this mystery.

"You haven't told me anything that will help me find these people," I told him.

His head dropped and he looked like a puppy that had just peed on the rug. "I'm sorry."

I suggested he focus just on the women. "Is there any way you can tell them apart?"

He took a deep breath, then let it out. This time his eyes focused on something past my head. I even turned around to see what it was, but nothing presented itself.

"Is one of them musical? I see a piano keyboard."

"Beats me," I replied. "What does it mean?"

He put his hands to his temples and rubbed giving his best swami imitation. Phony, I thought.

"The black keys are all shiny and new but the white keys are yellow and chipped," he said. "Does that mean anything to you?"

"I don't know," I said.

"Is one woman white and the other black?" he asked. "Because if that's true, then it feels to me like the black woman is the one who's fine, and the white one is not so fine. And one more thing. Didn't I read in the Minneapolis paper that a guy named Yuri turned up dead in a trash can somewhere out in the western suburbs?"

OK, maybe he wasn't a total phony, I thought as I headed the car west on Interstate 94. Maybe BJ had pulled up Pace's hand. Then I turned to thinking about her empty mailbox. I was just getting off at the Fifth Street exit when it dawned on me. Duh! Somebody was taking in her mail for her. I just had to find out who that was and hope he or she would let me sift through it.

I drove back to her apartment in Linden Hills and stuffed one of my cards into Pace's mailbox. On the back I wrote, "If you're taking care of Pace Palmer's mail, please call me."

Chapter 31

I sipped my brew as I stared into my computer screen, trying to give Thom the impression that I was just about to break the story of the decade. My cell phone rang.

"This is Lefty," said the gravelly female voice on my phone.

"Lefty?" I said.

"Yeah. Your card was in Pace's mailbox? Whaddya want? I'm a busy ninety-year-old. Don't know how much time I got to do what I gotta do. Ninety is old, you know. "

I explained I was looking for Pace and wanted to rifle through her mail, while in the back of my mind I was thinking I liked this lady already.

"Better come now," she said. "Tick tock."

Minutes later I pulled up to the same curb, stepped over the same pile of snow, but dirtier, and entered the same condo building. This time I pressed the button for Lefty Lathario, who buzzed me in immediately.

I looked around her overstuffed condo. A gong at least six feet across served as the demarcation between the living and dining areas. Some kind of wooden carved Aztec, about six feet, which I guessed was Lefty's height, stood in one corner. Every inch of wall space, going up at least to Lefty's reach, was covered with photographs. I recognized a few places. Machu Picchu, Lake Como, Hanoi. The rest were lost to me, but they captured a range from a frozen tundra to a majestic mountain to desert sands.

"You like to travel, I see."

"Yep," she said. "Next stop is Kuala Lumpur. But you're not

here to talk about my travels."

"You're right," I said. "Tell me about Pace."

"Pace was supposed to be back August 18," Lefty said. "I don't know what's happened to her. I'm worried. I take in her mail every day after I deliver the newspaper."

"You deliver the *Citizen*? At four in the morning?"

"Yeah, that's how I recognized your name. I've been reading the paper every day since I learned to read," she said, pushing her magnifying eyeglasses up on her nose. "Delivering gets me out of bed and there aren't many cars on the road at that time, so the driving's easy. Keeps me busy. "

I peeked around Lefty's large bony frame to see envelopes neatly sorted on her dining table. "Can I see Pace's mail?"

The biggest pile was circulars, from Bed, Bath and Beyond, Pottery Barn and Target. Bills from Penny's, Herberger's and Macy's, plus Comcast and T-Mobile, composed the next pile.

She watched me eyeball the mail, then directed me to the smallest pile. "This is the interesting stuff."

What looked like a letter from a law firm topped the pile of personal mail. "You could do federal time for opening somebody's mail," Lefty said.

I picked it up and held it to the light. It looked like there was one typewritten sheet of paper inside. I couldn't tell what was written on it.

"Not if she's dead."

Lefty let loose with a deep belly laugh, the kind of laugh that guaranteed a long life. "S'pose you're right," she said.

It's a cliché to steam open an envelope so no one can tell it's been opened, but that's what we did. It's also melodramatic to open a letter with fingernails, rather than tips, to avoid leaving prints. I did that too.

The letter, from an associate at one of the biggest law firms in town, said attorneys there would have to decline to meet with Pace to discuss her planned lawsuit due to a conflict of interest. It was dated August 4, the day Pace left on her vacation.

"The firm represents DRS," the letter said.

Lefty was looking over my shoulder as I read.

"DRS," Lefty said. "That's where she works. They make something called BabySavr. Keeps infants from dying in their sleep."

We both read the letter again, with Lefty moving her lips over every word. "Damn, that girl," Lefty said. "Pace wants to sue her boss. Didn't know she had it in her."

The postmark was August 4, so it arrived in Pace's mail probably no sooner than August 6, after Pace was gone. We looked through the rest of her mail to see if anything else might hint at what was going on with Pace, but there was nothing. That's the problem today, I said to Lefty. People seldom send good old-fashioned letters written on paper with ink.

Why would Pace sue BabySavr, I wondered aloud. The most obvious answer was gender discrimination. But I hadn't gotten any hint of that from all the people I had interviewed. Was there another reason?

"I think I know what that was about," Lefty said. "Pace is very private person. But she's lonely, too. I just hate to see a young woman like that with no one to talk to, so a while back I said to myself, 'Lefty, that Pace needs a friend, even if it is a tattered old broad like me.' Anyway it was a Saturday night about a year ago and I kinda invited myself to her kitchen and we started to talk. I could tell something was bothering her. Finally I got it out of her. BabySavr was hurting older kids."

"How?"

Lefty said Pace had been following up on records of teens who had used BabySavr when she began to notice a pattern. A lot of them died in the H1N1 pandemic.

"She said she tried to tell the big boss but he wouldn't listen. Something about a DPO, QPO, IPO? I don't understand business."

"It's an IPO—initial public offering," I said. "Means the company plans to go to the stock market to sell shares to raise money. The company wouldn't want bad news to scare away buyers."

"Pace told me she had to find a way to stop the company from killing any more kids," Lefty said.

Chapter 32

I stared at Lefty a moment, while taking in the rest of the scene. For the first time I noticed a birdcage covered with a red-and-white checked cloth in the corner of her small living room. "You've got a bird?" I asked.

"A parrot. Name's Bucky, for Buckminster Fuller," she said as she to stepped to the cage and yanked off the cloth. "Say, 'Hello, Bucky.' "

Right on cue, the bird blinked its big black eyes at me and squawked, "Hello, Bucky." Then he let out a laugh that was a digital-quality reproduction of Lefty's.

I watched him reach up on his claws, then give his wings a big flap as though tossing crumbs from a tablecloth over the balcony. As he settled down I thought through what Lefty said about Pace. If I were Pace I would have done all my research on a computer at home.

"Do you have a key to Pace's condo?"

"No, but I think she kept one in the glove compartment of her car," she said.

"Wanna help me try to get into her condo?" I asked.

"I'm always up for a little skullduggery," she said.

I grabbed my down jacket while Lefty stepped to her closet where she pulled on galoshes, a long wool coat and a fuzzy hat. "We can go out this way," she said, pointing to a door to the garage.

Pace's car, glued in place atop the parking ramp by ice, was the one with the Wellstone and 'Proud American' bumper stickers. Snow still covered a third proclamation that said, "Once a ..., always a ...." I brushed the snow away to reveal that the hidden words were "nurse."

I tried all the doors in the unlikely chance one was unlocked. No luck.

Now I really was faced with a problem. Breaking into her car was illegal. But I'd already opened her mail, plus stolen that tape from the truck. What was one more venial sin?

Lefty pulled a straightened coat hanger from her sleeve with a smile and handed it to me wordlessly. This was the point where I was glad my brother had shown me how to open locked car doors, just before he was arrested. Seconds later I was rummaging through Pace's car, wishing mine were as neat. Maybe you get to keep your car free of odd French fries, gas receipts, and soccer balls if you don't have kids, I mused.

"I don't see any key here," I said to Lefty. "I don't even see any lint."

"Let me try." She reached under the front passenger seat and pulled out a key box that had been held magnetically to the springs. "What about this?"

Minutes later we were in Pace's immaculate, plant-free condo. I made straight for the laptop on the secretary just inside the door. On TV the snoop always has to go through several tries to guess the password. I was hoping that Pace felt as secure in her home as I did in mine, and didn't bother to put a password protection on her own laptop. I was right.

"This is where you got me," Lefty said, her hand on my shoulder as she peered at the screen. "I don't even know how to turn those things on."

I tapped into the file named BabySavr, which was slim, but tantalizing. It included letters to two law firms in town asking for representation in a suit against BabySavr. One was the big outfit that turned her down. The other was a solo practice. She included citations to various medical journal articles as possible alternative explanations for the deaths of the sixteen teens who had used BabySavr to keep them breathing as infants. Although her letters referred to attached materials, I couldn't find them anywhere in the file. She made it clear she thought there was a connection between the teens' deaths and the device. She ended with this: "Still, it is statistically significant that so many of the lives BabySavr saved have ended so early. We must look into this immediately."

I emailed the entire file to my personal account, then searched everything else on her hard drive and backup, looking for anything that related to the company. Zip. Nada. Zilch. Finally, I erased any record that I had been in the file, a trick my smarter brother who has never been arrested taught me.

"Lefty, I think we've made some progress," I said, as I shut down the laptop. We locked up Pace's condo, leaving it just as we'd found it.

"Am I going to see this in the newspaper I deliver tomorrow?" Lefty wanted to know.

I assured her that, no, it would be awhile before I had this sorted out enough to put it in the paper.

"I'm gonna be watching for it every morning," she yelled to me as I walked down the hall toward the elevator.

"Great," I replied. "Why don't you hold onto Pace's condo key?"

Lefty replied with a smart salute.

When I got back to the office I printed out the whole shebang, stuffed the papers in a file and headed to my favorite hiding spot, a coffee shop in what was once the baggage storage for the now-defunct Milwaukee Railroad depot. It's a couple blocks from the newsroom and not connected by skyway, so seldom frequented by editors. I needed time to sit, read Pace's file, and think. In a tight newsroom, it's not good to be seen just thinking. On the phone or typing are okay. But thinking, no. The bosses see thinking as a waste of time.

The file was a good get, but frustrating. There was no documentation to back up her charge. I couldn't believe that conscientious Pace, the meticulous research director, didn't have papers stashed away somewhere. But where?

So what, exactly, did I have here? One of two women whose body might still be in Lake Harriet had suspected that her employer was responsible, at least indirectly, in the deaths of sixteen children. That was clearly enough for a story, except that I had obtained the information through means that were on the shady side of the law. Steaming open a letter is tampering with the mails. I wasn't sure snooping through her computer wasn't illegal, too, but I didn't want to find out. Nope, I needed to use the legitimate information I had to ask questions and lay my hands on data legally. I also needed advice from somebody who knew business.

As soon as I got to the newsroom I headed back to the business department to talk with my buddy who had covered medical device companies since the stethoscope was invented, it seemed. Her quip was quick when I asked her what she knew about BabySavr.

"Ask your husband, he wrote the last piece about them," she said.

"Can't," I said.

"This must be good," she replied. "What's up?"

"With Michael or BabySavr?"

"Both."

"Michael and I are separated. One of my 'missings' worked or works at BabySavr. "

I didn't tell the reporter, Maureen McCarthy, Pace was thinking about suing BabySavr, because she would have begun working the phones looking for a story. I didn't need that complication. As it was, she had already picked up some chatter from a researcher at one of the big stock brokerages about BabySavr's plans to go public.

She gave me the name and phone number for the researcher and I gave her a rain check on coffee because I didn't want to discuss Michael with her. After all, he is her competition and I didn't want to give her an unfair advantage over him.

I called the researcher and confirmed that BabySavr had planned to sell shares late last summer.

"But they pulled back without giving a good reason," the researcher said. "It didn't make any sense. The company was doing great. Selling like crazy with plans for new products. There's a reporter at the St. Paul paper, Michael Marks, who's been following them carefully. He would know all about it."

Geez, I thought. I just can't get away from the guy.

I left a message on Pace's supervisor's phone, hoping she would call me back so I could ask her why the company had retreated from the stock offering. Then I dug out the BabySavr annual report, copied the pertinent pages, re-filed the report and returned to my desk to study the copies.

I studied the picture of the principals again and my eyes fell upon the Hunk, which reminded me that he hadn't returned my phone calls from earlier in the week. Not uncommon. Doctors are notorious for not returning reporters' phone calls.

I pulled out my sheet of phone numbers and started dialing. Found him on the third try, which was quicker than I had expected. I explained who I was and why I was looking for Pace.

"What makes you think I'd know where she is?" he asked.

"I thought you were seeing her," I replied.

"I don't know where you got your information, Sweetheart, but it's wrong."

Whoa, I thought. That doesn't jibe with what I had heard.

"But you are on the board, correct?"

He allowed as how he was and seemed quite happy to talk about the company. He told me he had been with the company going back to the earliest days. Then he waxed eloquent about the BabySavr.

"We've got an ancillary product in the works, too," he said. "This is one hot company."

I asked him about the decision to withdraw from a public offering.

"It was some legal technical snafu that didn't mean anything," he said.

"Did you know anything about Pace suing the company?"

"What? You're kidding, right?" His voice got hard, his pronunciation very crisp. "Where did that come from?"

"I can't tell you that."

"It's a lie. Whoever told you that is lying." He suddenly begged off the phone, saying he was getting paged. But not before he added, "We'll be going to the market in the spring. You might want to buy in early. This company is going to be big, very big."

Chapter 33

"I'm outta here." I logged off my computer with a nod to Slick and Dick.

Feet in my Uggs, hands in my mittens, head in my hat I sat in my car letting it warm up a minute or two before I left the ramp. While I sat there, I reviewed what I knew about Pace Palmer. She seemed to be a good woman who didn't deserve to die. She had quit nursing for fear her MS would cause her to drop a baby, for crying out loud. She had told Lefty she was worried about BabySavr killing kids. Was the hand BJ pulled out of the lake hers? If it was, what happened to her?

Sometimes when I'm deep in thought I can drive from point A to point B without actually noticing what I'm doing until I get there. Then, I can't remember what happened after I left point A. This time I was thinking about Michael. Mid-career, mid-thirties is an awful time to watch the dissolution of the industry that has been not only your livelihood but your passion.

But I'm in exactly the same spot professionally as he is. Why didn't I react the way he did? Why didn't I want to chuck us? I wasn't sure.

I started in the news business thirty-six years ago, in utero. My mother wrote a weekly column for our neighborhood broadsheet, the paper of record for winners of best pet contests at the neighborhood park and the beacon for those eager to know about planning and zoning changes. It was her only chance to sit down while trying to keep peace among my five brothers. She said I was born with a genetic instant response to sirens, not only because she liked to chase them, but because my father was a fireman. In fact, that was how they met.

Growing up was a rough-and-tumble affair. I learned early that fun was whatever my brothers were doing, so I made it my business to wriggle my way into their impromptu wrestling matches and pickup baseball, football and hockey games.

From their point of view, I was a pest. Such a pest, in fact, they stopped calling me by my given name of Marguerite when I was about four, and started calling me Skeeter while swatting me away like a mosquito. It was good training for a reporter.

Even today I've been known to play a little one-on-one basketball with my brothers. Fortunately, I have long legs. Unfortunately, the 150 pounds on my five-feet, six-inch frame slows me down.

At sixteen I took over my mother's job writing for the local rag in the summers and worked on the school newspaper fall to spring. My senior year I had a falling out with the nun who advised the paper, and vowed to get out of journalism forever. I went to the University of Minnesota with a major in biology and plans to go to medical school. But the math was beyond my ken, and soon I was working for the campus newspaper. I haven't managed to extract myself from the business since.

Anyway, next thing I knew I was sitting in the parking lot just opposite the bird sanctuary on the northeast end of Lake Harriet on the edge of Lakewood Cemetery.

Although the bird sanctuary is meant as a stopover for migrating warblers in the spring and perfectly safe during the day, people have been attacked there at night. I've told my girls a hundred times that if they go in there alone at night and come out unscathed, they'll still have to deal with my wrath for doing something so stupid.

I looked around the parking lot. Not a car in any of the other thirty or so spaces. Surely no one else would be in the preserve tonight. It was too cold to be outside for very long, and heaven knows the crime rate goes down in the winter because the riffraff have left for warmer opportunities. If Pace, or somebody, died near here, I needed to look around if I was really going to understand this story. On the other hand, going there alone in the dark was a risky choice.

I decided to leave the decision to fate. I'd reach under the front seat, and if I found a flashlight it would be a sign that I should check out the preserve. If there was no flashlight it meant I should just go home and have dinner.

Pulling my left mitten off with my teeth I groped under the front seat. I felt a small flashlight. OK, I thought, maybe I need another sign that says whether I should go. If the battery works, I'll go. If it doesn't, I won't. Seemed simple. I moved the little slide on the flashlight until the sucker lit up like a Bic at a rock concert. Time to go.

When I opened the car door the overhead light flashed bright and the bell chimed so loudly that I caught myself saying Shhhhhhhhh as I slammed the door and locked the car.

Then I mentally took a step back and looked at myself. What was wrong with me? I never would have been frightened before. Never would have left my decision making to fate. All this stuff with Michael had thrown me off my game. I chastised myself and pushed on.

Dogs aren't allowed in the nature preserve for fear they will disturb the birds. The entrance is enclosed by an eight-feet-tall chain link fence and a turnstile with interlocking metal teeth that allow only one person to enter at a time. I gave the gate a little push and the cold metal-on-metal squealed like a stuck pig. It took a little more pushing to get it to move enough to let me in.

The bird sanctuary is about thirteen acres of bog. Fresh snow hadn't fallen for a few days and apparently a few folks had tromped down the path, packing the snow. Even though there were no leaves on the trees, the branches formed a thick canopy that would have blocked out any light from a moon, had there been one.

I was about forty feet down the path when I began to question why I was there. What had led me here? Was I somehow communing with the spirit of the hand in the lake? I don't believe in that sort of thing, but something had definitely pulled me there.

If I wanted to get rid of somebody, this is where I would do it, I thought. The dead-and-buried in adjacent Lakewood Cemetery wouldn't tell. Nor would the fallen trees or the bog or the birds. And the deep, dark center of Lake Harriet is the perfect place to dispose of a body.

I let the beam of the flashlight play over the ground as I walked. Freeze-dried leaves, hard cold bark, and the occasional cigarette littered the ground, reminding me that I really wanted a smoke. I kicked what I thought was a clump of ice in frustration. Why had I promised my girls that I would never smoke again?

The ice block turned out to be a boulder that barely moved and it hurt my toe, even through my boots. I shouted in pain and sat down on the rock to take weight off my toe, and to think. The boulder was seriously cold on my butt so I didn't stay long, but as I rose I saw that I had moved it just a smidge, and there was something shiny under it. With my good toe I pushed away the snow and leaves to reveal a hypodermic needle. Heroin is cheap and plentiful in the Twin Cities, and here's another piece of evidence that it's everywhere. Somebody's been shooting up in the patch that's supposed to be devoted to nature, I thought. I didn't want some kid to find it so I picked it up gingerly and headed back down the path.

I was almost to the edge of the sanctuary when I heard a car engine start. The turnstile's squeak seemed twice as loud as I pushed through one more time and caught the taillights of a small yellow car pulling away. Odd, I thought. There weren't any cars there when I parked. My heartbeat quickened. Maybe I should have paid more attention to the feeling that told me this was dangerous.

I unlocked my car and shoved the key in the ignition, again letting it run a bit while I blew on my fingers through my knit mittens. Then I rummaged around under the seat until I found an old Styrofoam coffee cup to serve as a receptacle for the needle, which I then shoved in the glove compartment. I figured I'd throw it in the trash when I got home.

Staring out the window while the engine warmed, my eyes fell on the metal racks where people keep their canoes in summer. The stands were empty now, but by early spring they're usually full of canoes. Some are locked, some are not. I wondered if the unlocked ones are sometimes stolen. People in Minneapolis are trusting souls. I bet that the canoes rest there all summer, free for the taking.

Chapter 34

I took the scenic route around the lake and headed home. I hung my jacket on the peg by the door and took the back stairs to the upper unit in our duplex. I rapped gently on the door and stuck my head in the kitchen of our tenant, friend and sometime childcare provider Helmey (rhymes with tell me) Andersen. Suzy was seated at his kitchen table finishing some math homework that was well beyond me. Helmey was pinching the edges on a piecrust.

"Dad will be here for dinner tonight," Suzy said, then, looking up from her work, "How was your day?"

"Not bad. Yours?" I stole a piece of apple that hadn't made it into Helmey's pie.

"Katie and I aren't best friends any more," she said. "She's best friends with Jenna now."

"She can't be best friend with both of you?"

"Mom," she said, "BEST is the superlative of the word good. You can't have two BESTS."

"So how do you feel about Katie?"

"It's okay," Suzy said. "I'm best friends with Peter now."

Glad that that was taken care of, I turned to Helmey. "Pie looks great."

"I made two. One for your dinner, one for mine."

"You're the best, Helmey," I said. He gave me a wink and a smile.

Suzy, Rebecca and I were seated around our kitchen table just about ready to dig into the stew left over from the night before when Michael pushed open our back door. When the temperature is in the double digits he bikes to and from work. He had his helmet tucked under his arm and his messenger's pack carrying his work clothes strung across his back. Frost had accumulated on his beard. I stole a look at his nice, still-tight ass in his long biking pants.

"Sorry I'm late," he said, slamming his stuff on the floor under the table as he pulled out a chair. "Smells good."

We four ate in silence for a while, then Michael cleared his throat. "So, what's new?"

I took that as a signal this was going to be a night when we would all pretend that everything was normal, that Michael lived with us, that our marriage wasn't in question. Fine with me.

"I got an A on my math test and Rebecca is getting her tongue pierced," Suzy said. "Isn't that going to hurt?"

"It's not going to hurt because it's not going to happen," I said to Rebecca.

"Dad?" Rebecca mumbled with a mouth full of stew.

So much for a meal from the good old days.

Suzy looked up from her plate but said nothing. Michael reacted as he always does in tense situations. The muscles in his jaw tightened and the artery on the side of his neck jumped out and began to pulse visibly. He narrowed his eyes to a laser point and stared at Rebecca. He was forming his response, I knew.

Michael put down his fork then placed his hands on either side of his plate.

"Rebecca, you are fourteen years old. You're old enough to decide what you want to do with your body."

"No," I said, "You need to be eighteen or have a parent's permission to get your tongue, or anything else, pierced. I'm not giving my permission. When you're eighteen, you can do whatever you want."

"Then Dad can sign. Right?"

"Dad's not going to sign anything," I said.

"You let her push you around, Dad?" she asked.

"You are not going to play us off against each other like that Rebecca," I said. "Leave the table. Now."

The rest of the meal continued without fireworks and Michael stayed to help with cleanup, rearranging the dishes I'd just loaded into the dishwasher.

"I'm not going to give Rebecca permission for piercing anything," I said. "Green and blue hair is enough rebellion for this week."

He wiped the counters while I put away the food.

"We've got to have some ground rules with the girls," I said.

He threw the sponge in the sink. "Like what? Anything you say goes?"

"We've got to have a united front with the girls, even if we aren't together ourselves," I said.

"I think you're wrong. She should be able to make mistakes."

"Not if they threaten her health," I said. "Tongue piercings get infected."

"This isn't about her health." His voice was getting louder.

"What is going on here, Michael? A month ago you would have agreed with me that letting a fourteen-year-old pierce her tongue is insane."

"A month ago I didn't realize what a bitch you are," he shouted.

Had he slapped me it wouldn't have hurt more. If he was looking for a shock effect, he found it. He'd never talked to me that way before. Never called me a name. Never been so raw. What was worse, I was sure the girls had heard him.

"Get out of this house," I said.

Chapter 35

FEBRUARY 19

"Tyesha Thomas is here for you." It was the security guard calling from the front desk.

"Who?"

"Tyesha Thomas. She says you're expecting her. Says you're gonna give her a tour of the newsroom."

Amber's sister. I had totally forgotten she was coming. "I'll be right down to meet her."

Although she was tall for eleven, Tyesha was that wonderful mix of a little girl and an adolescent. She wore long arms and legs and a bright smile, combined with jeans and a hooded University of Minnesota maroon-and-gold sweatshirt under a black down vest. Her tennis shoes were no protection against the snow. She reminded me a lot of my Suzy.

"Glad to see you," I said. "How did you get here?"

"Bus," was her toothy reply.

"Do you take the bus a lot?"

"All the time. We don't have a car. Pinky had one for a while. She used to drive me wherever I needed to go. But she crashed it. And she's gone now, anyway."

As we rode up in the elevator people got on and I introduced her to each of them. She nodded without making eye contact. When the elevator doors opened and we stepped into the newsroom, her eyes opened wide, as though she were trying to memorize every detail.

Most of the newsrooms in the Twin Cities—newspaper, radio or TV—are overwhelmingly white. Editors at our paper have tried over the years to hire more nonwhites, and have had some success, especially with Hispanic and Asian reporters. But African Americans are few. I'm sure that didn't escape Tyesha.

"This is where the sports writers work," I told her with a sweep of my arm. Her head pivoted on her neck as she took it all in. Reporters, mostly guys, sat at computers pounding away. They tend to be early to mid-thirties, dressed in jeans and T-shirts or sweatshirts.

"Is everybody in sports the same?" she asked.

"Yeah, kind of," I said. "Except for that guy over there. He started here when he was in high school. I think he's almost eighty now."

"I want to be a sports writer," she said.

We ambled over to one of the rising stars who was putting the finishing touches on a piece about the new coach at the University of Minnesota's women's basketball team. "This is Tyesha Thomas and she wants to be a sports writer someday."

He pushed away from his desk and rose to his full six-feet, four-inch frame. "Do you want my job?"

She tipped back her head and looked him straight in the eye. "Yes."

He chuckled and shook her hand. "Wanna sit in my chair and see what it feels like?"

She sat gingerly, then twirled the phone cord in a circle. "Do you have to press nine to get an outside line?"

"Yep," I said.

"Can I type something?" she asked.

"Go ahead," he said.

She wrote "Tyesha Thomas Sports Reporter," then flashed him a big smile. He replied with a thumbs-up as she spun around in his chair again.

"C'mon Tyesha," I said. "Let's go look at the rest of the newsroom."

After the tour I returned her to my desk. "This is where I work."

"Cool." She surveyed the papers on my desk and noted the pictures of Pace and Yuri I had hung on the wall of my cubicle.

"Who's that?"

"They've gone missing."

"Where's a picture of my sister?"

"I don't have one," I said.

"How come you have pictures of a white lady and man but not Pinky?"

"Because I found one of them and I haven't found one of your sister yet." I was a little embarrassed.

"You coulda asked me." Her tone was haughty and her eyes burned. "My grandma says they only put pictures of black people in the paper when they kill somebody."

The comment hung in the air like a drippy, jagged icicle. I'd heard that complaint before and didn't know what to say.

"Do you have a picture of your sister I could have?" I replied.

She dug into the pocket of her jeans and hauled out a school shot of a handsome young woman with piercing black eyes and skin like the best Godiva has to offer. Her jaw was strong under a big smile, which looked a lot like Tyesha's.

"Did you carry around a picture of her before she disappeared?"

"No."

"Why do you have a picture of her now?"

"Because I'm afraid I'll forget what she looks like. You can have this one. I got one at home."

I thanked her and hung the photo on the wall, next to Pace and Yuri.

"Do you know where Amber is?"

"No," she said, looking me squarely in the eye.

When Tyesha told me she had to go to the bathroom, I directed her down the hall and told her to come back to my desk when she was done. I was engrossed in my reading when I realized she had been gone for twenty minutes. When I didn't find her in the bathroom, I hunted in the sports department. She hung up a phone just as I tapped her on the shoulder. "Come on."

She was treated to a front-row seat at one of the more argumentative news meetings. Fridays are often fuller news days because events tend to bubble to the surface at the end of the week. Today was no exception.

Seven stories and three terrific photos were vying for page one. There was a particularly gruesome murder in one of the western suburbs and a fire on the north side of the city accompanied by a spectacular photo. The President had delivered a speech that morning suggesting legislation that would have a huge impact on the economy. Our photographer had snapped a great shot of the chancellor of the Minnesota public college system sobbing at his own resignation. State legislators were fighting about how much money to spend on roads versus buses. One of the best writers in the newsroom had put together a hilarious piece about 3M introducing a new waterproof cast that is perfect for bathing with a broken leg. Good photo on that one too. And a foot of snow was forecast for tomorrow.

"Maybe we should run two front pages," the features team leader suggested.

"Considering the newspaper is bankrupt, we're lucky we get one front page," said the managing editor. "Ladies and gentlemen, I'm opening the bidding. Now's the time to secure your place on 1A tomorrow."

A dozen editors sat on mismatched chairs loosely arranged in a horseshoe around a whiteboard in the center of the newsroom. The managing editor, a tall blond woman with a long face that makes me think of a graceful palomino, stood next to the board, flipping a red dry marker in her right hand.

The education team leader pointed out that 140,000 students attend the public college system and would be affected by the chancellor's resignation. "And you can't beat that photo," she said.

"If he'd been fired, I'd agree," the politics team leader said. "But resigned? Not 1A. Now, all 5.1 million Minnesotans drive on the roads. That's a story for 1A if ever there was one."

"Snore, snore," snorted the public safety team leader. "The fire was a four-alarm. And the murders in the suburbs were right out of *In Cold Blood.* "

"So now we're a supermarket tabloid?" asked the features team leader, who was editing the waterproof-cast piece.

"TV will be all over the fire," public safety spit back.

"Even more reason for us to give readers something they won't get from *Eye Witness News*," features replied.

"People care about death and destruction," public safety retorted, "not political hacks or college administrators."

"Anyone else?" the managing editor wanted to know.

I glanced over at Tyesha, who was sucking up every word.

"A foot of snow. A FOOT of snow." Weather doesn't fit into any one news category, so responsibility for covering it floats. Today the general assignment leader claimed it.

"Yeah, and the last time we told readers the weather guy predicted twelve inches we got two. Made us look like idiots." After years of wrangling with cops, the public safety team leader is one of the most aggressive types in the newsroom.

"Haven't heard from you, Mr. Sports Editor," the managing editor whinnied.

"Hey, people look at the sports section first. Anything on 1A is just buried."

After the guffaws settled, the managing editor chose president, 3M cast, snow and the fire for 1A, with refers to the chancellor and fire, which would lead the second section. Roads went inside the second section.

"When she hits a pothole that knocks off a wheel, she'll run the next roads story 1A above the fold with a shot of the errant hole," said the politics team leader.

As the editors scattered to their desks, Tyesha turned to me wide-eyed. "Is that how it really works?"

"Yep, 365 days a year," I said as I showed her to where we had hung up her vest.

Tyesha was in the elevator when I headed for the sports reporter's area to thank him for being nice to her, but apparently he hadn't returned to his desk after she used his phone. I was a couple of steps away when something occurred to me. I hit the redial button on his phone then jotted down the number that played across his screen.

The phone's message system picked up on the half-ring. "Leave Pinky a message."

So Tyesha does know how to reach her sister, I thought as I left my own message. "This is Skeeter Hughes from the *Citizen*. I'm working on a story about missing persons and I'd like to talk to you. Can you call me back, please?" I left my office, home and cell numbers.

After my third cup of coffee, I was on my way into the ladies room when the cell phone clipped on my hip chirped. The caller ID was a Florida area code.

"This is Skeeter Hughes."

"You call me?"

My trip to the ladies room would have to wait a bit longer. "If you're Amber, I'm the reporter who called you."

"How'd you get my number?"

"Tyesha used a newsroom phone to call you. I hit the redial."

"Why?"

I explained I was working on an article about missing persons, and she was one of them. "Your grandmother is worried about you and Tyesha misses you."

"Why do you care?"

Oh, the possibilities of smart-ass remarks that ran through my mind. I'm curious whether she left her hand in Lake Harriet. Because she returned my call it's safe to assume she is not the dead person I think I'm looking for. I'm just a meddling reporter. Instead, I played it straight.

"The cops say two people are missing right now. One of them might have drowned in Lake Harriet last August. I'm thinking that's not you."

That pulled a deep laugh from her. "You're right, lady. I haven't drowned in Lake Harriet. In fact, I'm in Orlando while you are freezing your ass off. And I'm stayin' here."

"Your grandma and Tyesha would sure like to know you're okay," I said.

"You a social worker?"

"No, I'm not a social worker, but your grandmother seems like a nice lady who cares about you."

"You're not going to tell her where I am, are you?" The tough voice morphed into the whine of a girl who'd talked too much.

"It's none of my business," I said. "But from what I hear, you're a smart lady and you've got a full scholarship waiting for you. You could grow up to be Michelle Obama. Don't blow it."

"You're right," Amber said. "It's none of your business. But I know stuff that might help you. I heard something at Lake Harriet the night before I blew town. I'll tell you if you promise not to let my grandma know where I am."

She had it right the first time. I'm not a social worker and what she does is none of my business. It's not my place to share that kind of information with a family member, I thought. Plus, Tyesha obviously knew where she was. "It's a deal. When exactly did you leave town, and what did you hear?"

"I split August 4," she said.

My phoney-baloney antenna began to vibrate. "How do you remember the date exactly?"

"It was my birthday. I turned eighteen. Figured I was free and clear."

"What did you hear?"

"Me and some friends were sitting in a car near the bird sanctuary partaking a little blow, if you know what I mean," she said.

"Yeah, I know what you mean."

"Anyway, it was raining like some huge bladder had burst."

Did she have to choose this particular moment to talk about a burst bladder? "If it was raining, how did you hear anything?"

"We had the windows rolled down, OK?"

"OK. What did you hear?"

Cars on a highway, the rush of air and a passing truck played in the background of her call. When I heard the wail of a siren, I feared that some cop would pull her over before she spilled her info. But then the noise passed her by.

"A guy and a girl fighting. Then I heard her scream. It was just like in the movies, loud and long."

"Did you see anyone?"

"I told you. It was dark, raining. I saw nothing."

"Are you sure it wasn't just the blow that made you think you heard a scream?"

"Look, lady. I don't care if you believe me or not. I'm jus' telling you what I heard. Now you remember our deal. Don't you go talking to my grandma."

"I told you, it's a deal."

"Could you hear what they were saying?" I asked, but she had already hung up. I slipped my phone back into my pocket and completed my mission in the restroom. Washed my hands before I left.

I knew an investigative reporter who once told me to beware of sources who may have an ulterior motive. If your mother tells you she loves you, check it out before you believe it, he said. Amber wanted to keep her whereabouts unknown. That was plenty of motive to hand me a line of bull.

I checked our files for the weather forecast for the night of August 4. There was a 90 percent chance of rain that night, we told readers. Then I rifled through the notes I took from the list of missings in the police file. Thomas, Amber, DOB, August 4, it said.

Maybe she was telling the truth.

Chapter 36

Now I knew that Yuri was double-handed dead and Amber was on the lam in Florida. That left Pace as the most likely candidate for the hand pulled from the lake, if indeed it had actually happened. When in doubt, ask an editor, has long been my mantra.

"Yo, Thom," I yelled. "Talk?"

We stepped into the little conference room, where I laid out what I had.

"So, since we reported the last story that the fisherman said he found a hand, all you know is that it wasn't the Russian or the black woman, right?" Thom said, pushing a strand of hair behind his ear. "Seems like it's taken you a lot of time to come up with not much. We're going to need a story within a couple of days or you'll have to let this one sit for a while and work on something more likely to produce."

It wasn't the kind of inspiration or direction I was looking for. I didn't want to walk away from this story. My gut was telling me that there was something there. Intuition, reporter's DNA, whatever. I couldn't tell Thom about the psychic, or he'd laugh, then throw me out of the newsroom. But I had to come up with something.

"I'm pretty sure Pace Palmer was thinking of suing BabySavr," I said.

"How do you know that?" Thom asked.

"I'd rather not say." Actually, I'd rather no one knew I opened her mail, a letter from a big deal Twin Cities law firm, no less. Or her computer. "Also, BabySavr was all set to do an IPO last fall, then canceled."

"Companies pull back from IPOs all the time," Thom said. "Doesn't necessarily mean anything. But you think Palmer had something to do with it?"

"She thought, or thinks, the company is related to the deaths of sixteen kids," I said.

His eyebrows shot up, then he gave me that look through his half-squinted left eye, a look I'd seen before. It's his 'I'm-skeptical-but-intrigued look.'

"How do you know that?"

"Can't say," I said.

"Skeeter, tell me you didn't do anything illegal."

"Me, Thom? You think I might do some snooping that bends the law? How could you think such a thing?"

"OK," he said with a sigh, hauling his lanky frame from his chair. "Two more days. We need a story, soon."

Whew. That was close, I thought. I went back to my cubicle and stared at Pace's picture again. Maybe it wasn't the story I thought it was in the beginning. Maybe it wasn't that Pace was missing. Maybe she was sitting in New Zealand still trying to decide what to do, or even unable to face what she thought was the truth. Maybe it was bigger than that. Maybe the story was about a company that purported to be saving kids' lives but killed some kids instead. Maybe this was more of a business story than a missing persons story.

I had to retrace Pace's steps, find the kids who had used BabySavr and later died. The online database of death certificates requires the name of the deceased, which I didn't have. Presumably, Pace was starting with a list of names and addresses of patients who had used the device as infants across the U.S. and Europe. I didn't have that list, and doubted the company would share it with me. The U.S. Food and Drug Administration would probably have the information, but getting it would require filing a request under the Freedom of Information Act. Even if the FDA was willing to give me the names, which I doubted, FOIA officials can take months to reply.

Frustrated, I decided to take a break and check my Facebook page. I'd joined six months earlier ostensibly to have another way to communicate with my daughters on their own turf. Suzy thought it was "cool, Mom" but Rebecca saw it as an unwanted infringement on her way of life and snooping, to boot. She agreed to be my friend, but set a privacy shield that prevented me from seeing anything she or her friends posted to each other.

Much to my surprise, I found that several of my cohorts, some from college and even high school, already had Facebook pages. I friended them all, which helped me keep track of where they lived, what their kids were doing, who was married/divorced, and whether they were having a good day. Just for the hell of it, I put out a search for Pace Palmer. Well, look at that, I said more to myself than anyone else. Pace has a Facebook page. Much to my surprise, her page sported a link to her blog.

I clicked on it and began to read. I waded through a lot of stuff about nursing and what movie she'd last seen, what books she'd last read and recipes that sounded complicated. Then I came to an entry from last spring that said,

It feels like Doc Cobb and I have known each other forever. Met when I was a first-year nurse and he was a medical student. We'd grab coffee in the hospital cafeteria when either of us had a break, which wasn't all that often.

Not really sure why I see him. Maybe because he's entertaining? He's smart, too, and he knows it. But he's not a dedicated health professional. He always has a scheme that would make him rich. For Christmas I got him a T-shirt that said, "Trust me. I'm arrogant." He just laughed.

We went our separate ways after a few years. He had a residency in Portland and I moved to the neonatal intensive care unit at Women's and Children's Hospital. I loved working with the newborns, maybe because I can't have children of my own. Then I found out I have multiple sclerosis. Damn. Damn. Damn. It meant an end to working as a nurse. I would never risk dropping a baby.

But while working in the unit I watched BabySavr protect the lives of tiny babies whose respiratory systems were undeveloped. Then a sales representative told me the company was looking for someone to coordinate research on a similar product. I applied and got the job! It was a way to stay in medicine without worry about doing any harm.

The second day at work I saw Doc in the company's hallway. Turns out he's on the board of directors.

But the best was this entry from August 4.

I need time to think. Leave in the morning for a two-week trip to New Zealand, alone. Gonna walk the shores, see the sights, clear my head.

I can definitely feel fall in the breeze. Stared at my closet for a full two minutes trying to decide what to wear. What to wear? The Eileen Fisher celery sleeveless linen top with matching pants and a white sweater? Or the Jones New York denim pants with navy and white horizontal striped cotton shirt, the one with three-quarter length sleeves? Think I'll go with Eileen.

Looking forward to dinner at one of the small neighborhood eateries followed by a midnight stroll around Lake Harriet with Doc tonight. That's been our pattern all summer.

I headed home feeling quite smug that I had yet another piece to the hand-in-the-lake puzzle. That should have been a sign. When will I learn that smug always comes around to bite me in the butt?

Chapter 37

After Michael left I was determined to find a perk the girls and I could enjoy on Friday nights. Our routine, of late, had been to order a pizza and settle in for a chick flick, a cozy way to unwind after the week. I was careful to keep it low key. Neither the girls nor I needed any more stress while Michael figured out what he was going to do with our life together. I checked our Netflix queue before leaving the office and expected *The Blind Side* with Sandra Bullock to be in the mailbox when I got home.

The red-and-white envelope with the DVD for the movie was nestled between the Macy's circular and the phone bill when I retrieved the mail. As I dumped it all on our oak dining room table, I heard the chug, chug, chug of the washing machine, not something I was used to on Friday evening. Then I looked around and found a box of desk stuff—pictures of the girls, a coffee cup with the St. Paul paper's logo, an old pica ruler—on the floor next to Michael's jacket. The moment he stepped from the kitchen, I knew something was wrong. He ran his right hand through his hair, then stuck his thumbs in the pockets of his jeans.

"The paper laid off twenty people today," he said. "Including me."

He said it quietly, with a note of resignation in his voice. We'd both seen this coming, had talked about it for months. We'd shaken our fists at the money-hungry shareholders, wailed about the others who'd been laid off before, wondered how they would muddle through. Such a loss of knowledge for an industry whose very product was information was a shortsighted management blunder and a tragedy, we'd said. Then, we'd both gone to work a tad smug that it hadn't hit us. Until now.

"I'm so sorry, Michael." What else could I say?

He said the big editors had sent out an email right after deadline asking five reporters, five photographers, and ten copy editors to step into the big conference room. They said the last round of buyouts hadn't cut the staff enough. Free classified ads such as Craigslist on the Internet were sucking the newspaper's lifeblood. Why would people buy ads in the paper when they could sell their stuff faster and at no cost on the Internet?

"They said they were sorry, and we had half an hour to clear out our stuff while security guards watched," he said. "It was demeaning."

I wanted to go to him, to hug him, to tell him it would be all right. That he would find work that he enjoyed, that made him feel that he was productive, contributing to the common good, as he had at the newspaper. But his body language was stiff and I sensed he wasn't ready for my touch. And, frankly, I didn't know whether he would ever find work that meant as much to him as what he had been doing for the past fifteen years.

"What are you going to do now?" I asked.

"Laundry," he said.

"Then what?"

"I don't know. What are you guys doing tonight?"

"Pizza and a movie. Wanna stay?"

"I guess."

Moments later the girls came home, Suzy through the door first, followed several minutes later by Rebecca. They came home on the same bus, but Rebecca often hung back on the one-block walk home, seemingly in need of more emotional and physical space between home and school.

"Daddy!" Suzy said as she saw Michael. "What are you doing here? You said you weren't coming back until next week."

The scene was even sadder than when I watched it the first time around. Michael plopped in the chair by the window, his hands rubbing his thighs as he told her he had been laid off from the newspaper. "Oh, Daddy, I'm sorry," Suzy said, crawling into his lap.

Rebecca's reaction was less delicate but just as heartfelt when she heard the news.

"That really sucks," she said.

"Yeah, it does," he said. "Wanna dig through my stuff and take a souvenir from a dying industry. There's a pica ruler in there, I think, and a very dull Exacto knife."

Rebecca didn't much care, but Suzy snatched the ruler and a load of notepads with Michael's name and the name of the newspaper printed on the bottom.

After a while we called Domino's and ordered our usual—an extra large pizza with extra cheese, green pepper and mushrooms and a liter of Dr Pepper, then settled down for the movie. Michael started in on the twelve-pack of Grain Belt in the fridge and I watched Sandra Bullock's Academy Award-winning performance with one eye, and Michael with the other. He stared at the TV but I could tell he saw nothing. I knew this man, even if we were separated, and could see how his mind was working. He was mentally reviewing every decision he had made, probably going back to the day that he had decided to be a journalist. By the time the end credits were rolling I could see he had made a decision. I just didn't know what it was.

After the movie the girls went to bed and I cleaned up the detritus from dinner. Michael folded and placed his laundry in the plastic basket he was about to take to his car.

"I am sorry, Michael," I said as he shrugged into his jacket.

"Yeah, me too," he said. "Uh, remember when you asked me about the folks at BabySavr?"

"You said to be careful," I replied. "Something else?"

Michael half smiled, then reached into his pocket.

"Remember when I was gone so much?" he said. "It was because I was working on a story. This woman, Pace Palmer, came to me last summer and said there was something wrong with the company. She had tried to tell her brass and the FDA, but no one would listen to her. So she started to collect data on some of their studies. She said the company's device was actually killing kids. She wanted me to check it out. That was what I was doing."

After a while his editors thought he was spending too much time on it, and called him off to do other stories with a quicker turnaround.

"I had a weird feeling this morning something was going to happen at the paper," he said. "So I downloaded most of her information and my notes."

He pulled a thumb drive from his pocket and put it in my hand.

"Here," he said. "I no longer have a job that will let me print this."

Chapter 38

I couldn't decide which was more shocking, the coincidence that Michael and I were working on the same story or him handing me exactly what I needed to solve this mystery.

"Thanks," was all I could say.

"You're welcome." Carrying his meager box of desk stuff on top of the laundry basket of clean clothes, he hit the back door with his hip and stepped out into the cold. Through the kitchen window I watched the steam from his breath trail him to his car.

Heaving a sigh, I wondered what was going to happen to him, to us. Whatever demons he was already fighting, they would get bigger with the loss of his job. Considering his seniority at the paper, he had enough severance pay to last a few months. But then what? I didn't know, and I didn't want to think about it.

Instead, I slipped the thumb drive into my laptop and scanned the file. As I expected, Pace was thorough, meticulous, with page after page of documentation. BabySavr was first inserted in the lungs of tiny babies in 1987 during clinical trials in Europe, then in the U.S. Its use increased as its success grew. More babies lived than died. But as those kids reached their late teens and early twenties, becoming young adults whose lungs had reached respiratory maturity, problems began to pop up. Some of the patients were hospitalized for pneumonia. The illnesses became especially acute with the onset of H1N1 flu. According to Pace's calculations, sixteen of the 412 patients whose lives had been saved as infants by Baby Savr died, in some cases less than two decades later.

I stayed up half the night reading the file. I couldn't base a whole story on the research of a woman who was missing and possibly dead. But she included enough information I could follow. And, best of all, she provided the names and addresses of the kids who died, and another half-dozen who had been hospitalized. After grabbing a couple hours of sleep, I decided what Michael had given me was too valuable to hold until Monday. I called his cell phone.

"Can you be home with the girls this weekend?" I said. "I need to get to the newsroom."

"And it starts." He sounded groggy. "I'm out of work so I'm the babysitter."

"You don't 'babysit' your own children, Michael," I said.

He didn't reply, just showed up in the kitchen an hour later, as the girls were getting up. I gave him the schedule I had planned for the day: soccer practice for Rebecca, violin lesson for Suzy, a trip to Target for light bulbs, toilet paper and Tide HE.

"Coffee's made," I said as he looked in the refrigerator.

"You're out of half and half," he said.

"Then get some when you're at Target," I replied on my way out the door.

As I pulled the car out of the driveway and into the icy street I felt that wonderful surge of adrenalin, that sense that I was onto something after slogging through mud for way too long, the pure joy that comes when I know I'm on the right track. I knew that somehow I would find Pace Palmer, or at least figure out whose hand the fisherman pulled from the lake. Somehow, I knew the answer was tied to BabySavr.

Chapter 39

February 20

Downtown is eerily quiet on the weekends. No crush of foot traffic from the workaday crowd. I passed a guy whose job it was to vacuum the miles of skyway and then did a little hopscotch through the pattern sunbeams made on the cleaned carpet.

The newsroom was quiet, too, on this Saturday morning. The weekend crew hadn't shown up yet and the Friday night folks were long gone. It came as no surprise that the desks normally occupied by Slick and Dick were empty, except for the donut crumbs on Dick's computer stand. The last round of budget trims had cut the staff that emptied trash to once a week. Apparently, that day hadn't come yet. Wastebaskets overflowed with paper, Styrofoam clamshells and the occasional banana peel. At the far end of the newsroom I heard someone shout "Eeeeeeeekkkkkkk!" Newsy, the mouse, was back.

Sports reporters are always around, however, so I trolled in their area for a fresh pot of coffee. It's a cliché to call it sludge, but what can I say? It might have been sludge, but it was our sludge.

I slipped Michael's thumb drive into my computer, copied everything on it, then slipped it back on the key ring in my purse. Even though it had been years since the paper's computer system crashed, I wanted to be sure I had a backup of the information Pace had so painstakingly assembled. Then, to be doubly sure, I printed it all out on paper, 200 pages, which took about an hour. Then I started dialing for dollars. I called the public relations person at each of the forty hospitals where BabySavr had been used. Of course, none of them was in the office on a Saturday, but I left messages on every phone, asking them to call me back. I also called the office of every doctor named in Pace's report, leaving my phone number and the message "I'm working on a story about BabySavr and I'm hoping I can have fifteen minutes of your time to ask a few pertinent questions."

I was just trying to screw up the courage to call the families of the kids who died when I sensed a large figure in my peripheral vision.

"What are you doing here, Skeeter?" Thom asked.

"You told me I had to come up with a story pronto, so that's what I'm doing," I said.

"I'm already over budget on overtime," he said. "I can't pay you for this."

"I'll take it later in time off," I said, even though we both knew I wouldn't.

"I hear Michael was among those laid off in St. Paul yesterday," Thom said. "I'm sorry."

"Yeah, me too. Take a seat. I want to show you what I've got."

I fanned Pace's 200 pages in front of him and explained what was there. For the first time in a long time, I saw him lean back in his chair with a slow smile on his face. The tick in his eye was gone and he even refrained from tucking a piece of hair behind his ear.

"Good work," he said. "I'm not going to ask where you got this, but I'm sure you're going to verify everything that's here."

"Of course," I said.

"And then you're going to get some people not affiliated with the company to look at it and tell you whether it's valid. And then we'll get it edited and have the paper's lawyers look at it."

"You betcha," I said.

By the time we finished talking it was early evening. I decided Saturday night was not the time to be calling families who had lost a child. I'd put that off until Sunday.

I pushed the button for the elevator and waited for it to come, then retraced my steps through the skyway to the parking ramp. No dancing through a sunbeam pattern in the carpet this time, because the sun was long gone and I was too tired anyway. Only half a dozen cars remained on my floor of the ramp in the quickly fading twilight. Overhead lights programmed to turn on in the dark hadn't lit yet. I was ten feet from my car when I saw the problem. In my hurry to get to the newsroom I had shut the car door on the seatbelt buckle, leaving it slightly ajar the whole while I had been gone. The dome light was a dull gray. Apparently it had been on the whole time I was gone, draining the car battery, which needed replacing anyway. I stuck the key in the ignition and gave it a twist. Nothing. Not even a faint bleat. Dead.

True Minnesotan that I am, I always keep jumper cables in my trunk. But none of the cars parked in the ramp had occupants who could help me out.

Cold and in the dark, I dug through my purse looking for my AAA card. Couldn't find it. I squeezed my eyes shut tight and rubbed my forehead, trying to think. My mother always used to say when you can't find something, look under the bed. That wasn't an option, but I felt under all the seats. Turned up a cracked CD, an unfamiliar key and a wad of Caribou paper napkins, but no AAA card. Just then the overhead lights flickered to life. I was still cold, but at least it wasn't dark any more, so I looked under the seats again, and between the seats this time. Three French fries, an empty ketchup packet and two paper clips. Ahh, I thought. The glove compartment. That would make sense. There it was, the black-and-gold plastic card with my membership and phone number for road service. As the operator was telling me to stay with the car for about half an hour before the tow truck from Bobby & Steve's Auto World would arrive, I noticed the hypodermic needle stuck in the Styrofoam cup. I had picked it up at the bird sanctuary and planned to dispose of it, but forgot. Damn, I thought. I've got to do something with that. As I leaned down on the front seat to put the needle back in the glove box, I heard a vehicle approaching. Good, I thought, it's the AAA truck here to give me a jump. But then I realized I had heard the purr of that engine before—at the bird sanctuary. I poked my head up just a bit to peer between the seats of the car.

I must have picked up some of my brothers' car knowledge through sheer osmosis, because I can recognize some, like the Lotus that cruised by slowly.

My heart was pounding so hard I could feel the vibration in my ears. All my senses were suddenly set on acute. The dank, damp smell of road dirt mixed with melting snow and motor oil leaked months ago on the parking ramp concrete floor. The buzz of the lights overhead as the fluorescence flickered in and out. The screech of brakes and honk of a horn outside the ramp.

Like a trolling barracuda, with all its power in its jaws, the egg-yolk yellow Lotus moved sleekly up and down the mostly empty parking ramp. Once, twice I heard it circle the lot while I hid my head. When I sensed it approaching the third time, I stole another look just in time to see the driver's profile. There was no denying that curly brown hair, the finely sculpted nose, the jutting chin. It was the Hunk, Dr. Edsel Cobb.

What was he doing here? Was he looking for me? I figured one of the people I called just hours ago looking for comment had contacted Cobb. He or she probably told him I was nosing around about BabySavr. It happened all the time.

The rumbling of the tow truck must have scared him off because the Lotus disappeared.

"So you've got a dead battery, there?" asked the guy in the red-and-blue Twins cap and purple-and-gold Vikings jacket who jumped from the cab of the truck.

"Never have I been so glad to see a Bobby & Steve's truck," I said to him, as my heart began to slow a tad. "Did you see a Lotus leaving here as you came in?"

"Sure did," he said as he attached the charger to my battery. "That was some beauty. My uncle had one of those. Colin Chapman, the guy who invented the Lotus? Always one step ahead of the law. When they said he had a heart attack and died, people thought he really made it up and was sitting on a beach somewhere. Boy, those babies can handle. That one was an Elan, a two-seater coupe."

He went on to say that Lotus Elan was the car that Emma Peel drove in *The Avengers.*

"The British TV series? You watch that?'

"Yeah," he said. "In 2004, Sports Car International named the Elan number six on the list of Top Sports Cars of the 1960s."

He said Mazda looked at the Lotus Elan when it was designing its Miata in 1990.

"Most people in Minnesota would have the Lotus tucked away in a warm garage, covered up all cozy 'til the snow's gone," he said. "The guy driving that must have money to burn, or something to prove," he said.

"You gotta be kinda small to drive a Lotus," he said. "It fit my uncle snug and he's five-feet, eight. Production shut down in 1973. Anybody got one of those is somebody who likes to move fast, fancy and a little dangerous. That oughta do ya. Give her a crank, now."

I gave the key a twist and it started up right way. Then I signed the service slip and tipped the guy a twenty. Not only had he gotten me rolling again, but without intending to he had given me a perfect description of the Hunk.

Chapter 40

Okay, I know. I should have gone home. I should have called it a night, put my head on my pillow, closed my eyes, given my brain a rest. But suddenly, like my battery, I was recharged. One little piece of information that fits into a tantalizing puzzle does that to me. Sorry. I can't help it. It's just who I am. Plus, Michael was home with the girls.

I locked the car, making sure all the doors were shut tight and the dome light was off, and headed back to the newsroom. The night editors were in their places, the sports reporters tapping in final scores. The early mockup for Sunday's front page was half done on the layout editor's screen. OBAMA ON THE ROPES said the headline. This was news?

I made my way back to my desk and fired up my computer. My favorite picture of the girls flashed on the screen desktop, which always brought a smile to my face. I'll be home soon, I said to the picture, knowing it wouldn't be all that soon.

When I started in this business I would have asked a research person, who before that would have been called a librarian, to get on her computer and search a limited number of databases. The cost of her time and a per-minute charge for the database use would be billed against the newsroom budget. She might even spend some time looking through envelopes full of newspaper clippings about the topics I requested. But that was then. Instead, I logged onto the newsroom computer system and began to hit the search engines, inputting every possible variation for Edsel Cobb, tiger, Lotus Elan. I would need to remind Thom that doing the work myself probably saved the newspaper hundreds of dollars.

It was after midnight when I finished but I managed to dig up plenty about the Hunk. He's five feet, six inches tall, 180 pounds, with brown hair and brown eyes, the second son of a doctor and a commodities trader. He went to Breck High School, graduating in the middle of the class, then to the University of Minnesota in Duluth, where he majored in marketing. He graduated in six years and apparently took two years off. There was a gap in what I could find, but it appeared that he went to medical school at Wayne State University in Detroit, did a three-year residency in Portland as a hospitalist, then returned to the Twin Cities. He worked a couple of years in various hospitals around town, then started picking up work in urgent care centers.

I couldn't find anything that tied him to tigers, but that didn't come as a surprise. That was a shadowy business not likely to turn up tied to his name in any database.

But it looked like he was interested in more than medicine. In college he was a member of the marketing club and lived in a frat house. He wrote an editorial for the student newspaper titled "How to stash away a million dollars without really trying," predicting that one day the then-fledgling Internet would make the selling of body parts a very lucrative business. He was listed on several current networking websites and had been a member in good standing of the Minnesota Classic Car Club and the National Rifle Association for ten years.

Somewhere along the line he met up with the founder of BabySavr, investing heavily in the company. If my math was right it looked like he stood to gain millions of dollars if the stock offering for the company went as planned.

Was "the Hunk" a middling student who showed great interest in making money and had a penchant for guns? Or was he a well-educated professional who cared for the sick, especially children, and invested in stocks and fine automobiles, a patriot who believed in the Second Amendment? Was he all of the above? More to the point, did he have anything to do with Pace Palmer's vacation?

These questions played in my mind like socks tossing around in a dryer as I headed back to the car, which, fortunately, started up right away this time. I didn't know the answer, but I could feel in my bones that I would know, and soon.

Chapter 41

The drive home was quick and quiet in the early hours of the morning and I slipped noiselessly into the house. There's something about this time that appeals to me. The chatter of the day—emails, text messages, ringing phones—is gone. Especially in February, when snow and extra-paned windows muffle the whistle of the wind, I feel I can focus my thoughts. Maybe it's the faint smell of an old house, not as strong as mothballs, but there nonetheless. At times like this the scent of joy, anger, disappointment, surprise, expectation, frustration—life of a family—is strongest.

Both girls were asleep in their beds and Michael had taken a blanket and pillow to the couch, where he was sleeping fitfully. He always was one to talk in his sleep, sometimes carrying on lengthy arguments with demons I couldn't see. More than once I had to wake him before his shouting disturbed the girls, and even Helmey in the apartment above us sometimes heard him. Tonight I sat in the chair opposite the couch and watched as he punched the pillow and growled. The irony, of course, is that in his waking hours he seldom raises his voice.

His growl, sometimes rising to a leonine roar, made me think about Katya and Smirnoff. What did they have in common with Cobb? Did they have anything in common with him?

I got back online and fooled around with some more word combinations and databases. Came up dry again. Then, just for giggles, I put in Anton Smirnoff, the guy I met at Aunt Bea's who the feds charged with smuggling tigers, and People for the Ethical Treatment of Animals. It jumped out right at me like a lunging

German shepherd. Deep in a blog written by someone who also claimed to be a member of PETA was a hit list of top bad guys. A full-page picture of Smirnoff, standing with his boot heel on the neck of a white tiger, headed the blog. "Terrorist Tortures Tigers," said the headline on the blog.

Now, I seldom believe a word of what I read on blogs, especially those written by people I don't know, but, I've got to say, this was interesting. As far as I could tell, the picture had not been doctored. On the other hand, there was a picture floating around on the Internet for a while of Sarah Palin in a red-white-and-blue bikini with a shotgun resting on her hip that looked mighty believable until it was proven doctored. Still, I had seen with my own eyes the starving tiger both in the barn and on the videotape devouring the sheep.

According to the blog, Smirnoff imported tiger kittens and sold them to sports figures, bankers and big-money investors who used them as exotic pets. When the tigers grew too big to handle, or tore up somebody's Manhattan apartment, he drugged them and flew their bodies in caskets marked for fictitious mortuaries. He collected them with faked papers and delivered them to barns and sheds in small farm towns across the country where they woke up, plenty hungry. Once the tigers were back on their game he set up gambling operations: the tiger versus the sheep.

The more I read, the more I believed the blog. That videotape I found in the truck? I knew those guys were betting on the gory outcome. But here's what cinched it for me. The blog included a Google satellite map of Russia that looked exactly like the one I had seen in Katya's high-tech back office and on the computer of the tiger expert at the Minnesota Zoo. And then there was the fifteen-second digital clip of Smirnoff in the jungle. From the shocked look on his face, I guessed he had tripped the infrared wire and a camera intended to capture photos of tigers had grabbed his mug instead.

Katya and Smirnoff had already been arrested and charged in Yuri's death. A background piece on Smirnoff would give the story an interesting twist. But there were reasons why I couldn't write it. A sweet little woman who wanted to remain anonymous had shown me the satellite map. I had to protect her. And, I no longer had the tiger-devours-sheep-while-Smirnoff-and-Yuri-gamble tape, which I had stolen, a detail I didn't want to share with anyone.

None of it tied Cobb to Pace's disappearance, or her suspicions about BabySavr. A story about an employee who suspected a medical device company was responsible for several deaths was much bigger than a background article about a couple already charged with one murder. Still, I wanted what I knew about Katya and Smirnoff to see print. I decided to pass the tip to Slick and Dick.

I got a couple of hours sleep, got up, poured myself a bowl of Cheerios, then brought Michael a cup of coffee.

"I've got to go back to the newsroom," I told him in a whisper. "You're still here with the girls?"

"Fine," he said as he took the coffee with one hand while running the other hand through his hair. "What did you do to the bedroom?"

"Painted it." I really didn't want to have this discussion here and now.

"What were you thinking?" He tone was incredulous, not inquisitive.

"I was thinking the yellow was getting dingy," I said.

"So you went with I'm-depressed-please-shoot-me-now gray?" he asked.

"It's called Castle Moat."

"Skeeter, a dirt-cheap shrink would say you were making a statement about our marriage," he said.

"Maybe I was," I said.

"And you say I'm repressed," he said, then added, "Rebecca is seriously pissed at you. Can't say I blame her."

"Still?"

"Yeah, still," he said. "You'd better talk to her."

"I will," I said.

My eyes felt like somebody had thrown sand in them as I glanced over my notes again and stuffed them in a backpack to take to the office. Shrugging into my down jacket was an effort. What was I doing? Why did I work so hard? Why hadn't I gone into a saner and more secure profession, like computer programming?

Shouldn't I stay home and talk to Rebecca? More important, shouldn't I try to save my marriage? Shouldn't I go to Michael and say let's work this out? What do you want me to do? What will it take to keep us together? But I didn't. Instead, as I slogged through freshly fallen snow to the garage, I wished somebody would give me an accurate map to a happy marriage and a healthy career.

The garage door squeaked as metal slid on metal in the winter air, and the vinyl of the car seat was cold and crackly as I slid behind the wheel. When I turned my head to back out, the kink in my neck reminded me I had slept badly. The tires crunched the snow as I pulled the car down the drive. It was still dark.

Fortunately, the Linden Hills Dunn Bros coffee house was on the way to the office and had just opened. I had chugged a cup of coffee before leaving the house, but I needed something stronger to get all the parts of my brain working again.

"A depth charge, please," I said to my favorite barista as I surveyed the fresh pastries displayed at the counter, all made just hours before. "I'd like a chocolate croissant, but I had real problems getting my jeans zipped this morning," I said.

"My grandmother always told me, 'when in doubt, do without,'" said Jill Hurst, the woman behind the counter.

"That's why you're my favorite," I said to her with a chuckle. "You always give it to me straight."

"Have a good day," she called as I left.

Streetlights were just flickering off as I buckled my seat belt, pulled out of the parking lot and headed down 43rd Street, then hung a left. As I turned on Linden Hills Boulevard I noticed a car pull up in front of one of the smaller 1920s homes and an older woman scramble out. I was a hundred yards past when I realized it was Lefty, delivering the morning newspaper. Thinking about her made me smile and hoped I'd live long enough to be an old lady like her.

I decided to take the scenic route to the newsroom so I made a right on 42nd Street and headed down the hill to Lake Harriet. I was a quarter around the lake when I heard an engine revving behind me. I looked in my rear view mirror and spotted a flash of egg-yolk yellow. The Lotus!

Bam! The Lotus smashed into my right rear end. It packed a lot of power for a little bugger. It was a moment when time slowed down. My car careened then bounced off a tree, breaking off the rear view mirror and shattering the glass on my driver's side. I yanked the wheel trying to get control but on the freshly fallen foot of snow all I did was bounce over another curb. Then I tried to jam on the breaks but my snowy foot must have slipped off the pedal, because the next thing I knew I was hurtling toward the lake.

Chapter 42

Impact with the tree wasn't enough to set off the airbag, which was fortunate because it meant I could still see through the windshield. Gaining control of a spinning vehicle is tough enough on snowy roads, but when the snow is on top of ice it's impossible. I pulled the wheel in the opposite direction and the car rotated three hundred and sixty degrees. When I was a kid my brothers and I used to try the same trick in empty parking lots. It was fun creating donuts in the snow. But this wasn't fun at all.

The car spun around twice more each time, creating a curlicue that reached far onto the lake. When I stomped on the brake again it twisted into another skid. Shit, I thought, I'm going to hit that fishing house! I had a mental flash of BJ blithely sitting on an upside down bucket, dipping a fishing line through a hole in the ice. Before I could offer up a prayer to the god of ice fishing, the car slammed into the house, scattering rickety boards in all directions.

I felt the wheels of the car roll over the rubble, which slowed it down a bit, but not enough. It swung another one hundred and eighty degrees and suddenly I was going backwards, looking where I had been. Apparently no one was in the icehouse, because I didn't see any bodies left behind.

Finally, the car came to a stop. I sat for a second, took a deep breath, then rested my head on the top of the steering wheel. I was so dizzy I thought I was going to throw up. The caffeine I'd just ingested didn't help any. My scalp felt like it was full of sand, but when I scratched a bit I realized it was dusted with tiny pieces of glass. Blood dripped on my forehead. Wind whistled through the broken window.

Then I heard it, that clunk, clunk, clunk sound that the ice makes as it shifts across the surface, like the plates of the earth moving to and fro. It's deep, guttural and vibrates like a subwoofer from the very bottom of an abyss. Lake Harriet is spring fed and about eighty feet deep in its center, which was where the car and I had come to rest. Crunch. Crack. The ice was moving.

Not a week before, the paper had run a story reminding readers that the state requires all fish houses off the lakes by February 28. I couldn't remember what today's date was, but I knew it was after Valentine's Day, sometime at the end of the month. Although it had been a snowy February, the ice melt had already begun. Ice goes out in the center of the lake first. Was I about to be the lead in today's story of some idiot who drove on the lake when the ice was soft? I started thinking about headlines.

WOMAN LOSES LIFE IN LAKE ACCIDENT

REPORTER FOUND FLOATING IN SUBMERGED CAR.
FOUL PLAY SUSPECTED

or,

WHAT WAS SHE THINKING?
HARRIET TRAGEDY TAKES MOM'S LIFE

Before I could come up with another headline, the clunk of shifting ice plates changed to a high-pitched clink. Then crack, crack, crack as I felt one rear tire slip below the others. My car was falling into the lake, and me along with it.

Chapter 43

The rest of the nation may think it odd, but we Minnesotans drive on frozen lakes all the time, so firefighters here are well trained in car-falls-through-ice rescue. As the daughter of a firefighter, I'd heard innumerable conversations around the kitchen table about what happens when a car is submerged. The key piece of information is it's impossible to open the door until the pressure of the water inside is equal to the pressure outside. I sure didn't want to wait for the sucker to sink to get out. Nope, I had to open a window and climb out fast. Somewhere in all that spinning, the motor on my del Sol had stalled out. I tried to start it again to power down the windows, but no luck. Then I flashed on my father telling me about a small hammer intended to break a window in a situation like this. Buy it, he said. No, Dad, I said. I'll buy you one for your birthday, he said. I just laughed at him. Wished I hadn't.

I looked down and realized my boots were getting wet as icy water began to seep in. Bigger cars sink faster, my dad said. Once again, I was grateful that my tiny two-seater would float longer than say, a big, old SUV.

Again I heard my father's voice. If you go down with the vehicle and float away from the hole you may not find your way out. It's a very serious thing here in the northern states, he said.

Open the door, I thought to myself. Open the door and get out. But the temperature outside was hovering around zero degrees. My muscles just wouldn't follow the orders my brain issued.

Yank the latch above and take the top of the car, I told myself. Yet another advantage of a convertible. But again my muscles wouldn't budge.

I lifted my head and peered to the shore, where I saw Lefty's car and a woman waving her arms, shouting and pointing to what I could only guess was her cell phone.

I heard the wail of a siren. Then another and another. Of course, I'm accustomed to the siren's call. It usually gets my reporter's blood pumping. But it's different when you know the sound of approaching rescue is for you.

There's a station only a few blocks from the lake and four fire trucks were there quickly. Two rescuers in cold-water orange suits slid on their bellies across the ice, using picks to drag themselves along. On shore, two more orange- suited rescuers waited in case the first two didn't make it.

I've never felt so grateful in my life as I saw firefighters making their way carefully across the lake. Then, I heard it again—the clunk, clunk, clunk of the ice—and prayed that no emergency folks would be hurt. But I need not have worried. They knew what they were doing.

The first to make it to me was a guy who had worked with my dad before he retired and moved to Florida with mom.

"Jesus, Skeeter," he said. "What did you do? Wait till your old man hears about this."

I was too cold to reply. My mouth just wouldn't work.

Somehow, they busted the glass on the driver's side, got me out of there and bundled in a blanket in the back of an ambulance in record time. I closed my eyes and took a deep breath, thanking God I was still alive and promising I would live a good, sin-free life. I would never think bad thoughts about anybody. I would practice random kindness and senseless acts of beauty on a regular basis. I would pay it forward forever. Then I opened my eyes and saw Lefty talking to my favorite Minneapolis police sergeant, Victoria Olson.

"I saw the whole thing," Lefty told her. "This guy bashed Skeeter into the lake."

Olson assumed her oak tree stance, arms akimbo, feet planted twelve inches apart firmly in the snow. "Would you be willing to make a statement at the station about that?"

"Absolutely," Lefty said. "We're friends, you know, Skeeter and me. I'm telling you, I saw the whole thing."

When they hauled my car off the ice, Olson opened the trunk and tossed through my stuff—a bag of T-shirts I had intended to return to Target a month ago, the windshield wiper fluid, the can of dried paint destined for the recycling center. She opened the driver's door, brushed away the bits of glass with her gloved hand and poked her head in. Then she went around to the passenger's side, got down on one knee and looked under the car seats. She seemed to spend a long time in there. I watched in curiosity as she called another officer over to take a look. Then she went to her squad, pulled out a plastic bag, returned to my car and rummaged around for a while before returning to me.

"What's this about, Skeeter?" Holding the plastic zip lock bag by one corner she waved the hypodermic needle and the Styrofoam cup in front of my eyes.

She looked at me intently, as though she were trying to make a decision. Expressions of skepticism mixed with concern mixed with curiosity floated across her face. "Is it time for us to have a conversation?"

Chapter 44

"I know what you're thinking, and you're wrong," I told her. "I'm not using drugs. I found that in the bird sanctuary and intended to dispose of it. I thought it was left by someone doing drugs in there. I didn't want some kid to find it and get hurt."

"So why was it in your glove box?" she asked.

"Because I've been busy, okay? I hadn't found a safe place to toss it. And I forgot about it."

Sergeant Olson wanted to know exactly where and when I had found the needle.

"The bird sanctuary isn't known as a place where junkies shoot up, but it wouldn't surprise me," she said. "We'll run an analysis on this just to be sure."

The sun had come up in the course of all this and Sergeant Olson squinted into the horizon. "We have a damaged—actually destroyed—fish house involved here," she said. "I'm going to file a report. Are you willing to take a drug test?"

"I've got nothing to hide," I said.

"Good," she said.

"Now let's talk about the son of a bitch who drove me off the road and into the lake."

I told her the car was yellow and small, but I couldn't see for sure who was driving, even though I knew it had to be Cobb. And I told her about him cruising by me in the parking ramp.

"There's nothing illegal about looping by parked cars," she said.

Then she walked across the parkway to Lefty, who was sitting in her vehicle with the engine running. As Sergeant Olson approached, Lefty rolled down her window. Because she was facing me, and because Lefty's a little deaf and speaks loudly, I could hear every word she said.

"I was delivering papers when I saw Skeeter drive by," Lefty said. "I only had two more houses to go, so I finished those up and drove down to the end of the road. I was just gonna say hi to her, ya know? We're friends. Anyway, I was coming around the turn when I saw this car bash into Skeeter's."

I couldn't hear what Sergeant Olson said next, but Lefty's response was quite clear.

"I don't know what kind of car it was, but I'm positive it was black," Lefty said.

Olson said something else I couldn't hear.

"Medium size, I think," Lefty said.

Great, Lefty, I thought. She saw black. I saw yellow. She saw medium, I saw small. Olson was going to think we were both nuts. And that I was on drugs.

While Olson was talking to Lefty I began to warm up and got to thinking more about Smirnoff, and what I had read about him on the blog. Ever the reporter, I decided to take the opportunity to ask Olson a few questions.

"So SERGEANT, what's the current thinking among law enforcement about animal abuse?"

"What, exactly, do you mean, Skeeter?" she asked.

"I mean do you guys pay much attention to animal abuse? If you find, say, any links between animal abuse and other crime, for example?"

"Funny you should ask," she said. "That's turning into the cause of the moment."

Cops, she said, have long known that animal abuse is often about control and intimidation, but in the past five years the police and the Humane Society had begun to team up when they found examples of animals that had been treated cruelly. Increasingly veterinarians were asking harder questions about hurt animals and listening more closely to the answers. A study in the late 1990s showed that most women in domestic abuse shelters said their abusers also hurt family pets. Some had even delayed seeking help because they were afraid of what the boyfriend or husband would do to the dog if they left. The University of Florida even has its own crime scene investigators unit, she said.

"You mean doggie CSI?" I asked.

"Yep," she said. "Think there's a TV show about it?'

We both chuckled at the thought. "Why are you asking me about this? You know somebody who's got it in for Fluffy and Muffy?"

I told her about Smirnoff making the blogger's hit list of top bad guys.

"And you believe everything you read on the Internet?" she asked.

"Good point," I said. "But I saw some of this with my own eyes."

"Exactly what did you see?"

She listened carefully as I laid out for her exactly what I had seen in the shed. Well, almost exactly. I skipped the part about the swiped videotape.

"Bringing in endangered animals is a matter for the feds," she said. "But I know this much about the guys who do that. They're dangerous. Stay away from anybody who's doing that kind of thing."

I tucked that piece of advice into my noggin, then asked Lefty for a ride downtown to the newsroom. We drove silently. I just wasn't up to talking about anything. I cracked the passenger side window just a bit and felt the chilled wind coming through fresh and clean. Adrenaline was pumping through my veins and I'd never felt more alive in my life. When I got to the office, I went to the bathroom and combed broken glass from my hair. I even liked the sound of tiny shards as they fell into the wastebasket in the women's room. Colors were brighter, smells were stronger. I was alive, and very glad.

I even smiled at Slick, who was at his desk.

"What are you doing here on a Sunday?" I asked him.

"My job, Skeeter, my job. I hear you took a spin on the lake today," he said.

"Wow. You really are connected," I said. "What? You got a brain fuse with some cop?"

"Plain old listening to the scanner," he said. "Basic reporter stuff, ya know?"

This guy really needs to get a life, I thought.

"That doesn't explain why you're here," I said.

"I'm here because you need my help," he said. "Dick's on his way in, too."

Chapter 45

I must be in real trouble if Slick and Dick think I need help, I thought.

"What, exactly, are you going to help me with?" I asked.

"You're in way too deep on this tiger-and-the-hand thing," Slick said. "I know these people. Remember? They live down the road from me in Moose Meadow. You don't want to mess with them. I'm a reporter. I have my sources, just like you do. Better, really."

As if on cue, Dick pushed his way through the newsroom. When he pulled off his coat, I saw a pistol clipped to his belt.

Great, I thought. This is how I'm going to die, caught in the crossfire between Dick and a copy editor.

"You can't have a gun in here," I said to him.

"Do you see a sign that says 'The Minneapolis Citizen bans guns on these premises'?" he asked.

Unfortunately, he was right. Under state law, people with a permit can pack heat in public places and businesses, unless a sign says otherwise. As far as I knew, the paper had never had a need to keep out guns.

"Besides, I've got a license to carry," he said.

"Has that thing got bullets in it?" I asked.

"Of course," he said, hitching up his pants. "Never strap on unless you mean to use it."

"Just don't aim that thing at Newsie," I said. "I love that mouse."

Time was wasting. "OK, you guys," I said. "Here's what I know."

I filled them in on what I had read about Smirnoff on the PETA blog, and about the fancy satellite map. I even told them I'd borrowed and returned the movie Tony the Tiger Eats Mary's Little Lamb.

"That's pretty good work," Slick said.

"Looks to me like you manned up to this," Dick added with a chuckle.

"I can't man up," I said. "I'm not a man. But I can put on my big-girl panties and deal with it. That's what I did."

Then I told them I was headed back to Moose Meadow.

"You can't go there," Slick asked. "It's too dangerous for a girl. Right, Dick?

"You betcha," he said. "That's where we're headed. Don't even try to argue with us."

I didn't argue. In fact, I let them go. There were no more stories, at least for now, in Moose Meadow, I figured. Besides, it dawned on me as I looked at the demolished fish house that my buddy BJ was really the key to this. The best place to find him was on the ice.

Because my car had been hauled away to be fixed, I checked out one of the newspaper's cars and headed for Lake Harriet. Somebody had removed the remains of the fish house I had demolished earlier in the day. That left two on the lake, I probably because most people had heeded the state law and removed them in anticipation of the deadline. I guessed BJ's was the one with all the empty beer bottles scattered outside the door.

The lake is amazingly different in winter than in summer. When it's full of sailboats crisscrossing with the wind, it's almost alive, the waves moving like fingers, ducks paddling near the shore. In winter, like this day, it's an inert rock dropped into a hole.

But on this day sunshine made the ice and snow on the lake glisten so brightly that I had to shield my eyes as I walked. As I got closer to BJ's structure I could hear a radio blaring the hockey game, the Wild versus the Red Wings. Wild were losing.

When I knocked on the door it creaked open a couple of inches and I peeked in.

"BJ?"

"Whadya want?" he growled.

My eyes hadn't adjusted from the glare of sun on the ice to the dark drape of his inner sanctum. "It's me, Skeeter."

"Yeah?" he said.

"Can I come in?"

"Yeah."

I stepped in and stood a moment, squinting to take in the scene. It smelled like cold with a mix of fish, old plywood and old man. BJ sat on a white plastic upturned bucket, holding a foot-and-a-half-long fishing pole over a hole in the ice the size of a soccer ball. He had on a full-body caramel brown Carhartt body suit and big black rubber boots. His hands were red and chapped. The blade of a fishing knife glinted in light that seeped through a crack in his windowless shed. More beer chilled in the ice.

"I figured you'd be back." He didn't look up from the hole, just reached over and grabbed the neck of a beer with one hand while he held on to the pole with the other. He took a long pull on the beer, emptying half the bottle.

"Surprised it took me this long?"

"Yeah, kinda." A smile tugged at one corner of his mouth as he raised his rheumy eyes to look at me. My sight had finally returned and I could look at him more closely. I wasn't quite sure what I saw. Was he just some old guy fishing all alone on a cold day in February? Left with his thoughts and an icy posterior? Probably. But I thought there was more.

"Like my new ice auger?" he asked, pointing to the sharp-bladed giant screw he used to cut the fishing hole in the ice. "She's a StrikeMaster Lazer Pro. Got three-horsepower Solo motor. Cuts a hole ten inches across."

"Lovely," I said.

"Weighs in at only twenty-nine pounds, but she ain't heavy, she's my auger." He said it with a chuckle that morphed into a cough then a laugh so deep it took his breath.

"How do you know Dr. Edsel Cobb?" I asked.

"Wondered when you would get around to asking me that,"

he said. "Doc took care of my wife in the hospital. She died, ya know."

"You mentioned that," I said.

"He killed her."

"What do you mean, 'He killed her'?" I asked.

"Four words. He was IN-COMP-PE-TENT," BJ slurred. "Hospital fired him right after that, but they kept it real quiet. Never even made the papers or even the TV news."

I believed that. It had been years since there were enough reporters to keep tabs on things like that.

He stared at the red-and-white fish bobber floating on the slushy ice water of the fishing hole. "They're not biting today."

"I'm sorry, BJ," I said as I took a seat on a red plastic sled.

"After the missus was gone I was mighty lonely, ya know? Started hanging out at Mystic Lake. Those Indians sure know how to run a casino. Didn't have much more luck with the slots than I got with fish." He laughed, which turned into another hacking cough, which he assuaged with another slug of beer.

"One day I'm yankin' on the one-armed bandit and I see Cobb at the Black Jack table. He's rollin' and winnin'. I'm thinkin' you son of a bitch, why are you still livin' and my Loretta is gone."

"You wanted to kill him?"

"Yes, yes I did," he said. "So when he left the casino, I followed him."

The beer was coursing through BJ and I could tell he was having trouble keeping his words in order. It took about an hour—including the minutes he spent to step outside the fish house to relieve himself—but eventually I heard the whole story. "Like I said, I wanted to kill the bastard."

"But you didn't."

"No, but I coulda, ya know? But I seen enough killing in 'Nam. Didn't want any more."

We sat still in the shed and listened to the weather report. A low-pressure center was moving in. BJ turned off the radio in disgust. The only sound was the faint whistle of the wind.

"I started to follow him. Wasn't hard, him in that little yellow car, me in my old beat up Chevy truck. I'm just an old man, invisible."

BJ said he watched him wining and dining several women, even followed him to and from work. "I was on him like white on rice," BJ said.

Then last July Cobb started having dinner often with one particular woman.

"Kinda pretty lady," BJ said. "Tall, skinny. They walked around the lake after dark a lot. Looked like they were arguing lots of times."

"Pace Palmer," I said.

"I never knew her name. Last time I saw her they had dinner in the old-firehouse-turned-restaurant."

"Café Twenty Eight," I said.

It's one of my favorite places to eat in the neighborhood because I like to imagine firemen sliding down a slippery pole with a Dalmatian waiting beside the truck. When the bandshell burned down on Lake Harriet a century ago, rigs from this station probably answered the desperate calls. Michael and I ate there sometimes, in our better days. He always had the buffalo burger, I had the organic, locally grown chicken.

Servers at Café Twenty Eight are among the best informed in Linden Hills, because it's so small they can hear plenty while pouring coffee or wine.

"My grandson was hooked up for a while with one of the girls who works there," BJ said. "Always liked that girl, so I talked to her."

"You're quite the detective, BJ," I said.

"Do what I can. Anyways, she—that's my grandson's ex-girl—was pouring water for them when she heard that SOB say, 'You're out on a limb here.' Then she said, 'But what if it just made them worse? What if it killed kids?' Then he said, 'You don't have any proof.'"

BJ asked me if I knew what they were talking about. I nodded silently, then explained.

"Told ya he was a son of a bitch," BJ said. "Then they went to Sebastian Joe's for ice cream. I stood in line right behind the son of a bitch. He never even knew I was there. I tell you, I'm invisible," he said. "She got chocolate chip, the kind my Loretta always got. He got Rocky Road, I think. Then they pulled a canoe off the rack and paddled out to the center of the lake. Wanna beer?"

I declined his offer, then waited while he sucked down another. With the dozen or so empties outside and what he had in the fish house, I figured he'd gone through close to a case. My butt was frozen from sitting on the sled.

"Where was I? Oh, yeah. So I'm sitting under that tree hoping the lightning will zap Doc Cobb from here to Kingdom Come. I don't want nothin' to happen to the lady, but the fucker -- 'scuse my French -- needs to die. If it's by God's hand, so be it."

"I got my boat and rowed out, not too close, but close enough so I could watch what the son of a bitch was doing. She was in the bow. He was in the stern, paddling. Sorta like a gentleman, but he wasn't."

BJ said it was getting dark when a storm came up out of the west.

"All of a sudden, BAM, there's lightning. You know how they do, real fast like? Anyway, I started rowing like a bat outta hell back to shore. Wasn't gonna get my ass fried by some lightning. I was almost to shore when a big bolt shot across with a crack. I looked up to see it just as that son of a bitch was driving a needle into her butt."

"How could you see that?" I asked. "Were you close enough?"

"I told you, I got one bad eye, but the other one is better than most. I was a marksman in 'Nam, ya know."

"Maybe she was sick?"

"Nope."

I asked him how he knew.

"Because I heard her scream. Sounded like a bunny that the cat got. Then I saw him wrap her wrist with a rope to something big and heavy, like concrete, and slide her over the side of canoe. I heard the splash."

BJ said he went home and started a three-day drunk.

Oh my God, I thought. The Hunk really had killed Pace. He

drugged her, then drowned her. Her body must still be deep within the lake, maybe even under the very ice where we were right now.

And the hand that BJ fished from the lake? It must have been Pace's. Between August and October it probably decomposed enough to separate from the rest of her body where the rope was tied and floated to the surface, where it got caught on BJ's line.

I thought back to the needle I had found in the bird sanctuary. What were the odds that it was the same one Cobb had used to kill her? Pretty long, I thought. And the chances that BJ saw Cobb kill Pace and then by some fortune fished her hand from the same lake months later? Even longer. My phoney-baloney detector was vibrating at high speed.

"BJ, did you really pull a hand from the lake?" I asked, looking him square in his eyes, the rheumy one and the sharpshooter one.

He grabbed another beer, popped the top, then sucked the entire bottle down.

"Not exactly," he said as he let out a huge belch.

Chapter 46

"What do you mean, 'not exactly,' BJ?" I hate it when a source lies to me, even if it's something on the order of "not exactly."

"Look," he said. "I'm an old drunk with one good eye, a fishing pole and an old truck. Cobb is a young, fancy-pants doctor with a hot car and a lot of money. I know he killed my Loretta and I know he killed that lady in the lake, but nobody was going to believe me."

"But you thought people would believe you pulled just a hand from the lake?"

"Ma'am, nobody's ever accused me of making a lot of sense," he said. "But I thought that it would at least make the cops drag the lake. Then they'd find the lady's body and maybe figure out that Cobb did it."

"But BJ, a hand? Come on."

"Well, you know, long before you were born there was story in the neighborhood about some old guy who fished a hand from the lake," he said. "I guess it was one of those, whatcha call it, urban myths. Who knows, maybe it was true fifty years ago?"

He stood up to stretch his legs and wobbled a bit as he pulled on his crotch. "When the cops wouldn't even take the trouble to see if somebody really was in the lake, I was real frustrated, ya know? So I was out drinkin' with my boys one night and the one who went to high school with you said I should go to the newspaper about it. I thought, 'What the hell? Maybe she'll believe me.'"

He set his beer in the ice and reached out a nicotine-stained hand to help me up. I was tempted to have one of those beers, but

I knew it was the last thing I needed right then. As it was, I started screaming at him.

"I'm so pissed at you, BJ, I can hardly see straight. How could you do this? You lied to me. You wasted my time with the bullshit story and you made me look like an idiot to my boss, my readers and my colleagues. Why should I even believe you when you say Cobb killed Pace? You're probably lying about that, too."

My heart was pumping so hard I could hear it in my ears. But this wasn't from fright. It was from anger. All of a sudden all the crap that had happened—Michael leaving, Michael getting fired, Slick and Dick and their stupid remarks, the pressure from Thom to come up with a story or lose my job, trying to be the best possible mom to the girls—began to explode in my chest.

"You fucker," I yelled at him.

He looked down at his rubber boot and kicked a piece of ice. The red-and-white bobber started to move up and down. Looked like he'd caught a fish.

"I'm sorry," he said.

"Yeah, me too. I've got to go." I pushed open the plywood door to the shed with my right hand as I looked back at BJ, just in time to see a look of shock on his face, then feel a hard shove that pushed me back in. I tumbled back, twisting, twirling as my feet tried to grip but failed. My left hand, the one with the fingers that Katya had slammed in the car door, broke my fall as I heard my wrist crack. It sounded like a carrot stick snapping.

Dr. Edsel Cobb, aka the Hunk, blocked the door with his stocky body.

"Pleased to meet you, Skeeter," Cobb said. "I hear your fishing buddy figured it all out for you."

I looked at him closely, for the first time. Brown curly hair, brown eyes, square chin, just like in his picture. Not quite George Clooney, but close. Handsome guy, for a killer. Why is it that society has different rules for attractive people? It seems the more you fit the popular vision of handsome or beautiful, the easier life is for you. Strangers smile more at beautiful eyes, gorgeous hair, clear skin, a body with muscles in all the right places. Though unintended, the message to beautiful people is "You are good, even if you aren't."

"You thought you'd get away with this, Cobb," I said.

"Maybe. But there's no proof of anything. The old man here is just some sloppy drunk. I bet you don't even believe everything he said."

BJ's small fish house, the size of a small walk-in clothes closet, was getting smaller very fast. Suddenly it felt like a thousand vacuums were sucking away the little oxygen BJ and I hadn't already burned. The noxious mixture of stale beer, cigarettes and sweat that permeated BJ's ancient insulated fishing suit was almost overpowering. My heart pounded and my scalp began to perspire. My senses became so acute I could feel the fish swimming beyond BJ's hook.

Then I heard Pace's voice, the same one that had spoken on her answering machine the first time I called. It was coming from well below the ice. From that spot where the water still moved, where that clunk, clunk, clunk of shifting ice plates originated.

"It's him," Pace said. "He did it. Don't let him get away."

I promise you, Pace, I thought. He won't get away with this. Thoughts raced through my head as I desperately searched for a way that I could be sure he'd come to justice. What could I do? Just writing a story felt pathetic. Call Sergeant Victoria Olson and wait for justice to take its course? I knew that was the right approach, but it didn't seem like enough.

Cobb seemed to be fumbling with something in the pocket of his black leather jacket. From the corner of my eye I could see BJ appeared to be catatonic. Dammit, I thought, he's had too many beers over too many years to be able to move now. Cobb's eyes told me he had assessed BJ and come to the same conclusion. I was Cobb's primary target.

"I'm sorry," Cobb said, as he pulled a hypodermic needle from his jacket pocket.

But I was a step ahead of him. I pulled myself up and lunged for the fishing knife. Almost grabbed it in time, but my foot slipped on the beer-drenched icy floor. The move caught Cobb by surprise, I could see in his eyes. He was distracted for just a second, then pulled the plastic sheath from the needle with his teeth.

Chapter 47

In that moment I realized: this is it. I'm done. My earlier spin on the lake was just a taste of what death would feel like. What pissed me off most was I hadn't even had a chance to do all the good things I'd vowed I would do with a second chance at life. Then I heard it.

Vroooommmmm. Vrooommmmm. BJ came alive. With one hard pull on the rope, the gas-powered ice auger let out a roar loud as a jet plane.

"You're not going to get away with this, you son of a bitch," he shouted. "You killed my Loretta. You killed that girl in the boat. You're not gonna kill any more."

The blade spun around, slicing the air with a ferocious speed as BJ pointed it at Cobb's chest. Whirrrrrrrr. Whirrrr. Whirrrrr. BJ stomped toward Cobb, each step surer than the last. His body was straight and strong, giving me a glimpse of the jungle fighter he must have been in Vietnam. He was a man on a mission, both his eyes cleared, the set of his mouth a straight line over clenched teeth.

"Whoa, slow down there, buddy," Cobb said, suddenly shifting his focus from me to BJ. "You could hurt somebody with that thing."

"Damn right I could," BJ said taking a half step toward Cobb. "Shoulda done it long ago."

Cobb tried to back out of fish house, his palms held up in a fruitless attempt to ward BJ off. "Let's talk about this, old man."

"I'm not just an old man," BJ roared, waving the pointed end of the ice auger in Cobb's face.

Cobb backed up again, which put him outside the house. BJ took one long step until they were both outside, on the ice. Whirrrrrrr. Whirrrrrrr. The business end of the auger was inches from Cobb's chest.

"You may be a fancy, rich doctor, but you're evil," BJ tried to shout, but it came out as a slur, not from alcohol, but from anger, I sensed. He slammed his boot down on the snow, clipping the edge of one of the empty beer bottles. That threw off his balance and pushed him forward. Cobb tried to dodge left, but the blade of the ice auger caught on the zipper of his jacket. In a nanosecond it chewed up the leather and caught in his neck before the safety catch shut the augur off.

Blood gushed everywhere, crimson against the white ice and snow. In seconds the heat of Cobb's seeping essence, mixed with the icy cold, steamed over the ice. What looked like pink cotton candy grew on the snow. The hiss of air escaping from his sliced trachea reminded me of the radiators in our house when we bleed them every fall. The scene will be part of my nightmares for years to come.

There was nothing BJ or I could do to save Cobb's disgusting life. In less than a minute, his eyes were as frozen as the lake, his hand still clutching the hypodermic needle.

Chapter 48

Cops, firefighters, EMTs and their various cars and trucks littered the scene. Reflection from the ice and snow of the lake multiplied the blinking red and blue lights by about a zillion times. The same firefighters who had hauled me off the ice once already were back again.

"You know, Skeeter, your old man is going to laugh his ass off when he hears what you've done," said the EMT who had treated me the day before. Just his luck to get this weekend shift. "Then he's going to kill you."

I took a hard look at myself and I had to agree with him. The bruises on my fingers from when Katya had slammed them in my car door, oh so long ago, had turned purple-green. The shiner from yesterday's mishap had blossomed like a peony in May. It had been a while since I'd washed my hair and makeup was a distant memory. I couldn't recall when I'd ripped the knee of my jeans, but it might have been one of the times I slipped on the ice. What I had gone through to get this story was extreme, even for me, the dumpster diver. Still, I thought about swiping some of the yellow "crime scene" tape to use as a decorative item around my computer, but thought better of it. Maybe next time.

I guess the cold and the adrenalin sobered BJ because he was talking lucidly with my favorite police officer, Sergeant Victoria Olson. I ambled—limped?—over to hear what he was saying.

"... he killed that girl last summer. I seen it. After the bastard killed Loretta..."

"Slow down," she said. "What girl? Who's Loretta?"

I watched BJ's interrogation, admiring Olson's technique. Once again, I was struck by the similarity between the work of cops and reporters. Her questions were precise and she listened carefully to the answers, without reacting. But I knew that her blood pressure was climbing with every tidbit BJ gave. Like a burning building sucking in oxygen, the rush of the moment fuels the fire in us reporters and cops.

BJ repeated the story he had told me inside the fish house—the same one that Cobb had apparently overheard—with some added details that must have crystallized as the alcohol in his system dissipated.

He said he wondered about the hypodermic needle he saw Cobb stick in Pace's butt, and couldn't figure out why she didn't fight him when he tossed her in the lake.

"Seems to me she would have fought him, even if she was a nice lady," BJ said. "One night I was watching one of those CSI TV shows, don't remember which one. Anyways, the murderer used a drug that paralyzed some poor joe in minutes."

"It's called sucha something," he said. "That's probably the stuff he stuck in her, the SOB."

I'd seen the same show, then remembered reading about it. It's called succinylcholine, a muscle relaxant. As I recalled, it's used sometimes to make it easier for a doctor to stick a tube down someone's throat, and it can cut down muscle contractions during surgery. It can also cause your heartbeat to go wacko, stop you from breathing and jack your body temperature into the stratosphere. Dr. Edsel Cobb would have had easy access to the stuff.

Poor Pace, I thought. She didn't deserve to die so young, and especially not that way. She was a good woman, just trying to do what was right. Once a nurse, always a nurse, said the bumper sticker on her car. She died trying to be a good nurse. She suspected BabySavr was killing kids, maybe as many as it saved. According to the information she shared with Michael, she tried to go to the founders of the company to tell them what was wrong. When that didn't work, she went to the press, often the honest person's last resort. It must have taken tremendous courage to take that step to contact

Michael. How sad he never got to write the story, and she never saw it in print. Well, I would make that right, I thought.

Then I got to wondering. I'm sure Cobb got wind I was working on the story when I started making all those phone calls about BabySavr. He killed Pace. Would he have killed me—with the same muscle relaxant—had he found me when he was cruising the parking ramp?

Holy shit! Was succinylcholine in that hypodermic he had in his hand when BJ's ice auger screwed through him? Was the Hunk about to stick that needle in me? Did I narrowly miss a terrible death?

"Hey, Victoria," I shouted. "We need to talk."

She gave me a sign with her finger that said I should wait, but waiting is not part of my skill set.

"No. Now," I said to her.

"What can I do for you, Skeeter?" she asked.

"I think you'll find a muscle relaxant in that hypo the bloody pile of creep over there has, had, in his hand," I said.

"We'll have it analyzed," she said. "That reminds me. We got the analysis back on the needle that was in the glove compartment of your car."

"Already?"

"We do things quickly for our special citizens," she said. "It had traces of insulin in it. Are you diabetic?"

"No," I said. "I'm not a druggy either. I suspect somebody with diabetes was taking care of business and left the needle behind."

Olson nodded. "I'll need a statement from you, Skeeter, at the station."

Which is how I ended up in the back seat for a squad car for the second time in two days, and then had to call Michael for a ride.

Chapter 49

We drove to the newspaper's loaner car, which was still parked on West Lake Harriet Parkway, in silence. "It's over there, up about six cars," I told him, the only comment spoken between us for the ten-minute ride.

"Thanks," I said, getting out. "I'm headed home, if you want to go now.

But instead, he headed home, too. When I walked in the kitchen he was leaning against the sink.

"I've been putting out feelers for jobs," he said. "It doesn't look good."

"Can I take off my coat and sit down before we have this discussion?" I asked. I knew this talk was coming. I just didn't know where it was going.

Slowly, stalling for time, I kicked off my boots, took off my down parka and fuzzy hat, and made a pot of coffee. After it had brewed, I poured some in my favorite mug, along with several ounces of Kahlua.

"Want some?" I asked Michael.

"Just coffee, thanks," he said.

We sat in the living room as the February sun was sinking again, albeit a couple minutes later than the evening before, signaling that spring was en route, but still too long off. I was suddenly struck by the metaphor to our relationship, and started to giggle, which turned in a cathartic laugh.

"Now you're laughing at me?" Michael asked.

"Not really. It's been a tough couple of weeks, and, by the way, everything isn't about you, Michael," I said.

"OK," he said. "Explain to me what happened today."

I did. I told him about BJ's not actually pulling a hand from the lake. About how BJ had followed Dr. Edsel "the Hunk" Cobb because he thought Cobb killed BJ's wife, Loretta. How BJ witnessed Cobb murdering Pace Palmer.

"So BJ made up the story about the hand because he figured no one would believe he had actually seen a doctor murder a nurse. He wanted the cops to drag the lake, find Pace's body, and then, somehow, tie her murder to Cobb," I said. "But instead, Cobb started to follow me when he found out I was tracing Pace's steps. Then he overheard BJ, who'd had way too many beers, tell me the story."

I paused, took a sip of coffee to get my breath. I wanted to give Michael time to soak in everything that I had told him. And, I must admit, I was going for drama.

"Then Cobb came after me with his hypo," I said.

My hope was that Michael would put his arms around me, kiss my head and mutter into my ear he was glad Cobb had not succeeded, that he didn't want me hurt or dead. Instead he sat in our overstuffed chair, his hands on his knees, spread far apart. He scratched his thighs with his fingers tips, then patted them.

"And the dead furrier in the trash can? The tiger trappers? What does that story have to do with Crazed Hypo Doc?"

"Nothing," I said. "Turns out they were two totally separate murders unrelated to each other."

"I see Slick and Dick took the lead bylines on that one."

"It happens," I said. "You know that."

"What are you going to do?" he wanted to know.

"Write the best series of stories of my career, so far," I said. "Missing Research Director Claimed Medical Device Harmed Teens. Investor in Plymouth Firm Killed with Ice Auger. Hand Fisher Held in Incident."

"That's better than Alleged Tiger Trappers Charged in Murder," he replied.

"What about the missing high schooler?" he asked.

"As far as I know, Amber's still in Florida. But if her sister, Tyesha, hadn't called her, I wouldn't have known that. And if Amber hadn't told me about hearing Pace scream at the lake that night, I wouldn't have thought to go back to BJ."

"You always had good intuition about things like that, Skeeter," he said.

The silence hung between us again. Finally, he went to the kitchen for a beer. When he sat down across from me again, I saw tension in his face. He slugged back almost a full bottle of Grain Belt Premium before he spoke.

"Listen, I've called everyone looking for work. There isn't anything full-time and permanent out there right now, but I've got a ton of offers to freelance."

"Freelance is better than nothing," I said, slogging down the rest of my coffee-avec-kahlua.

"But I can't make enough money to pay rent and food by freelancing, so I was thinking I should probably move back in," he said.

"With me and the girls?"

"Well, yeah, what did you think?"

"If you're proposing moving back in because you can't pay the rent on freelance wages, well, that doesn't work, for me, or the girls," I said. "You said some awful things. You hurt me." But I knew his stated reason is often different from his real reason. Like I said, I know this man. "You said you didn't love me any more. You said you never loved me. You said you needed to leave to be happy. And now you want to move back in?"

"And you said you didn't buy it," he said with a smile. "Well, you were right."

"Meaning?"

"Meaning I'm glad your weren't killed or hurt today. You jump into your stories with both feet, so to speak. I know you're the dumpster diver, always have been, always will be. But I don't want you to fall through the ice in your car and drown. I don't want you to get stabbed with a muscle relaxant and I sure don't want you carved up with an ice auger."

It wasn't what I was hoping to hear from him. Nowhere near

enough. I waited.

"OK," he said. "I was going through an awful time. I said things I didn't mean. What do you want from me?"

"An apology."

He swished the bottom inch of beer in his bottle, chugged it down, looked long and hard through the hole, then raised his face to mine.

"I'm sorry." Tears welled up in his eyes.

"And I want you to bring home a chocolate truffle, every day for a week, just for me," I said.

He broke into a smile. "Done."

Epilogue

That was three months ago. The ice went out on the lake in March, just like it does every year. A couple days before Memorial Day, Pace's body washed up on shore, with her right hand attached to her arm. Apparently her left hand had actually separated from her body at her wrist where the Hunk had tied it to the concrete, even if BJ hadn't really pulled it up. I'm hoping the fish have disposed of it.

Amber's grandma wrote me a charming note that said Tyesha had talked Amber into coming home. "I don't know what role you played in that, but I'm grateful," she said. I'm looking forward to going to Amber's high school graduation in a couple of weeks. Her grandma says she's going to use that full ride to the University of Minnesota. I hope so.

The feds broke up the exotic animal business in Moose Meadow and the white tiger is living out its life at an animal shelter for abandoned big cats in a hidden refuge in northern Minnesota.

Katya and Smirnoff go on trial in the fall for Yuri's murder. The prosecution will say Yuri was out of the country buying furs when Katya reported him missing. (Apparently the videotape of Yuri I "appropriated" from the seat of the truck was taken long before he left on that buying trip. I should have known. Nobody uses videotape any more.) Katya was hoping Yuri'd never come back, so she could collect on his life insurance and run off with Smirnoff. That's why she wanted me to stop looking for him. But when he returned unexpectedly, and found that Katya and Smirnoff were getting it on, they killed him. It's a theory. Will the jury buy it? We'll see.

I'm still employed, for the time being, anyway. Slick and Dick continue to think a missing person's beat is a stupid idea, but they did acknowledge that I wrote "a helluva story" about Cobb, Pace and BabySavr, which the FDA pulled off the market.

And BJ, well, I found him recently sitting in a webbed aluminum folding chair on the shore, fishing pole at his side.

"I told ya," he said. "It was someone's hand."

The End